Q & RAY

· CASE #1 ·
THE MISSING MOLA LISA

TRISHA
SPEED
SHASKAN

ILLUSTRATED
BY
STEPHEN
SHASKAN

Graphic Universe™ • Minneapolis

For my sister Nicole, for introducing me to so many greats, including Sherlock Holmes, and for her continual support. Love you! —TSS

To my dad, who encouraged me to create art and collect comics —SS

Graphic Universe™
A division of Lerner Publishing Group, Inc.
241 First Avenue North
Minneapolis, MN 55401 USA

For reading levels and more information, look up this title at www.lernerbooks.com.

Main body text set in CCDaveGibbonsLower 11.5/13.25.
Typeface provided by ComicCraft.

Library of Congress Cataloging-in-Publication Data

Names: Shaskan, Trisha Speed, 1973– , author. | Shaskan, Stephen, illustrator.
Title: The missing Mola Lisa: case #1 / Trisha Speed Shaskan ; illustrated by Stephen Shaskan.
Description: Minneapolis : Graphic Universe, [2017] | Summary: "Quillan Hedgeson, a hedgehog, and Raymond Ratzberg, a rat, are students (and crime solvers) at Elm Tree Elementary school. When a theft occurs during a class trip to the local art museum, Q and Ray set out to solve the case, using their wits and a series of disguises" —Provided by publisher.
Identifiers: LCCN 2016009537 (print) | LCCN 2016032607 (ebook) | ISBN 9781512411478 (lb : alk. paper) | ISBN 9781512454147 (pb) | ISBN 9781512430226 (eb pdf)
Subjects: LCSH: Graphic novels. | CYAC: Graphic novels. | Mystery and detective stories. | Hedgehogs—Fiction. | Rats—Fiction.
Classification: LCC PZ7.7.S455 Cas 2017 (print) | LCC PZ7.7.S455 (ebook) | DDC 741.5/973—dc23

LC record available at https://lccn.loc.gov/2016009537

Manufactured in the United States of America
1-39653-21285-10/25/2016

WHO'S WHO

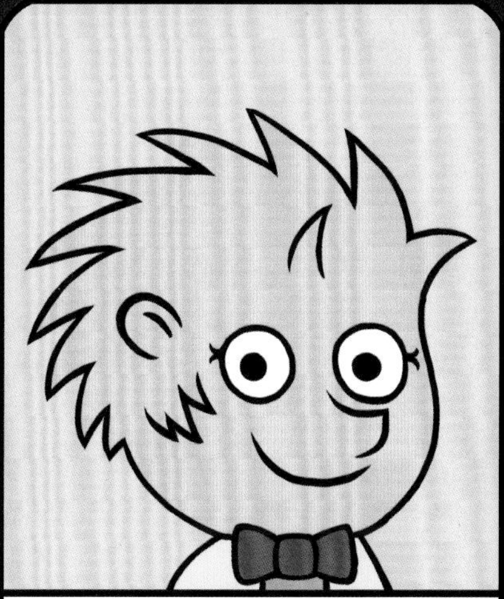

Quillan Lu Hedgeson
aka: Q

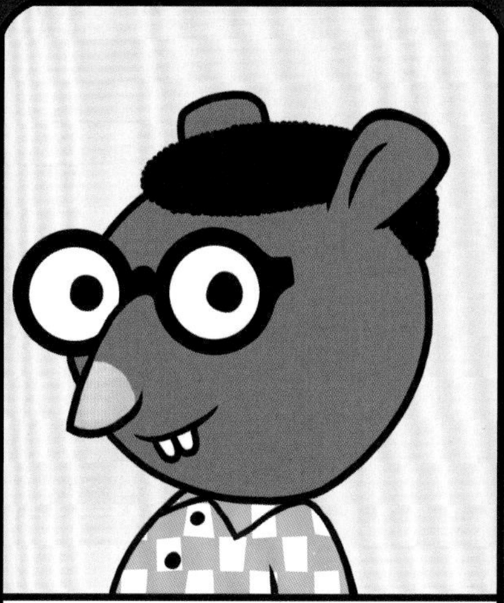

Ray Ratzberg

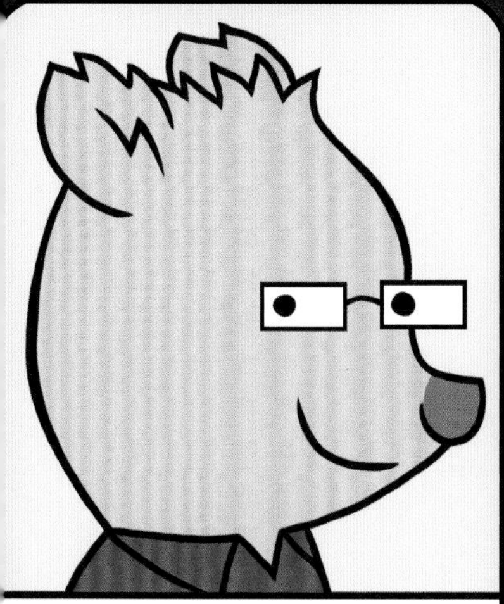

Mr. Shrew
Media Specialist

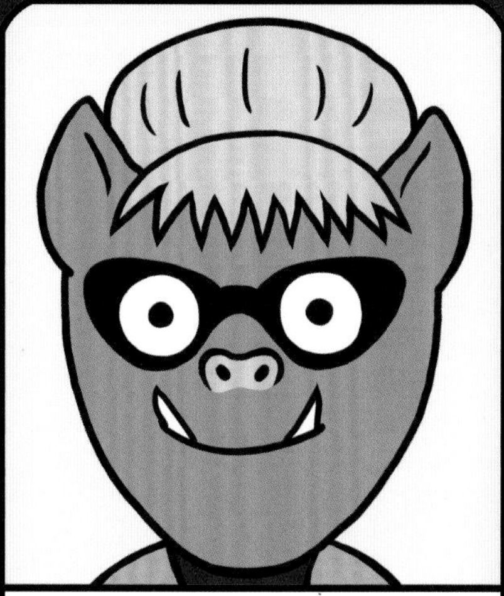

Ms. Boar
Classroom Teacher

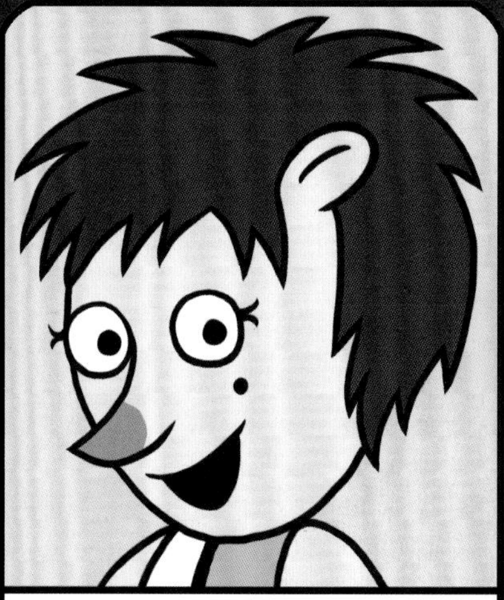

Ms. Easel
Art Teacher

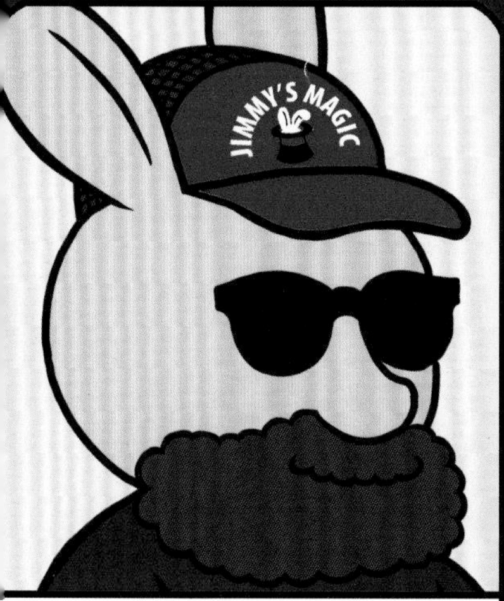
JIMMY'S MAGIC

Jimmy
Magic Shop Owner

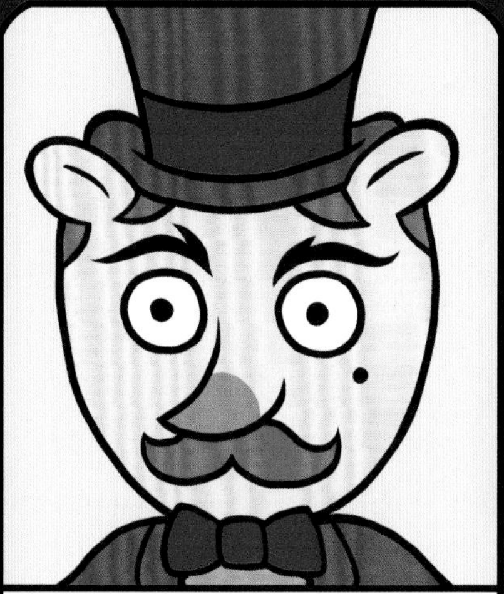

The Great Don Realo
Magician

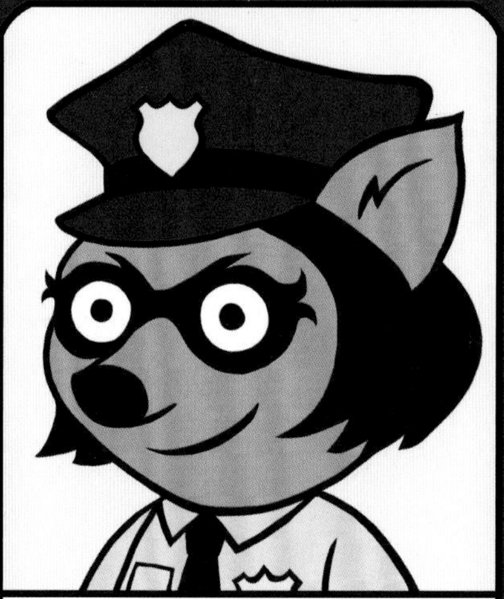

Officer Rocco

CHAPTER ONE
Q and Ray

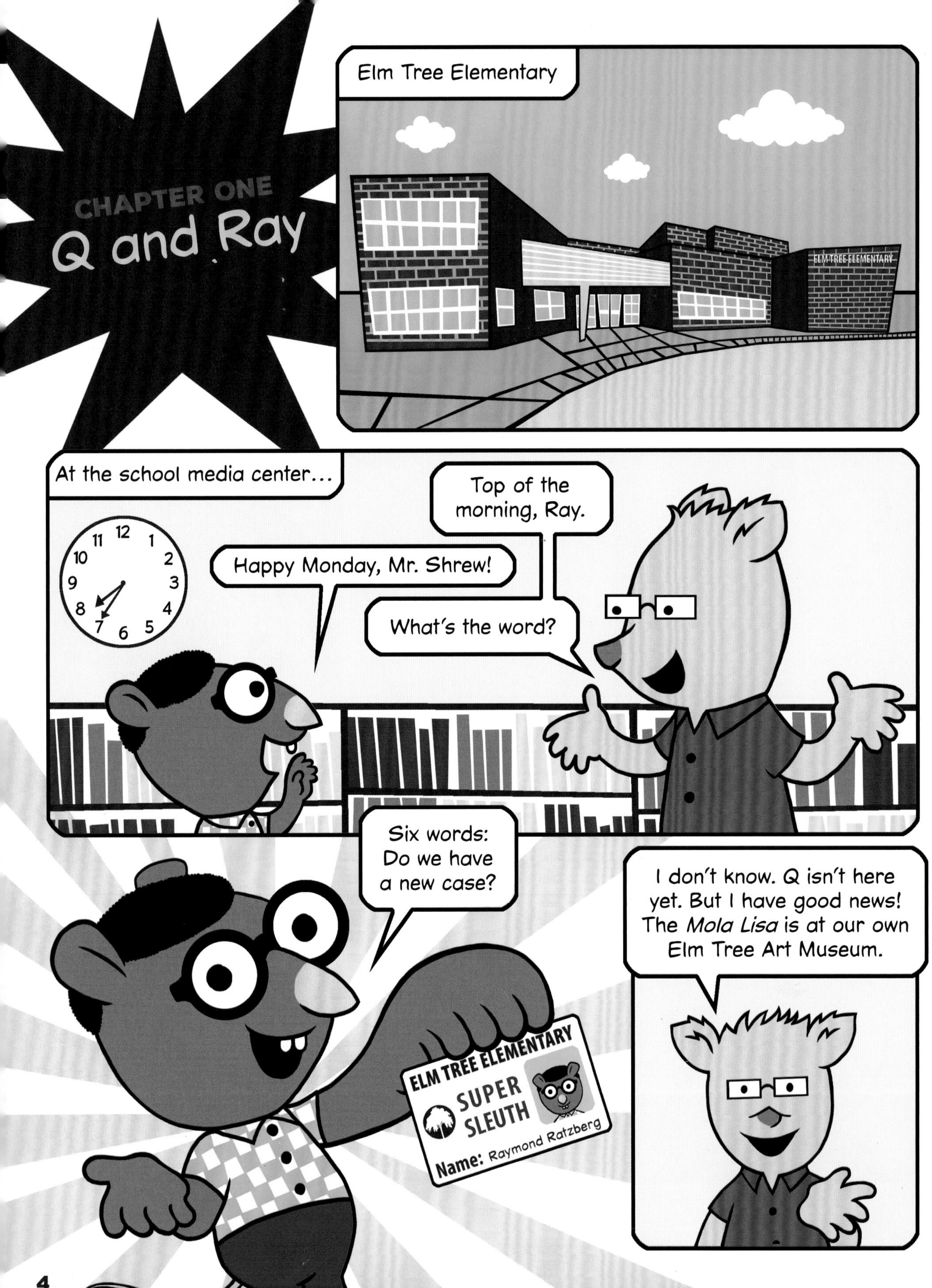

Elm Tree Elementary
ELM TREE ELEMENTARY
At the school media center...
Happy Monday, Mr. Shrew!
Top of the morning, Ray.
What's the word?
Six words: Do we have a new case?
ELM TREE ELEMENTARY
SUPER SLEUTH
Name: Raymond Ratzberg
I don't know. Q isn't here yet. But I have good news! The *Mola Lisa* is at our own Elm Tree Art Museum.

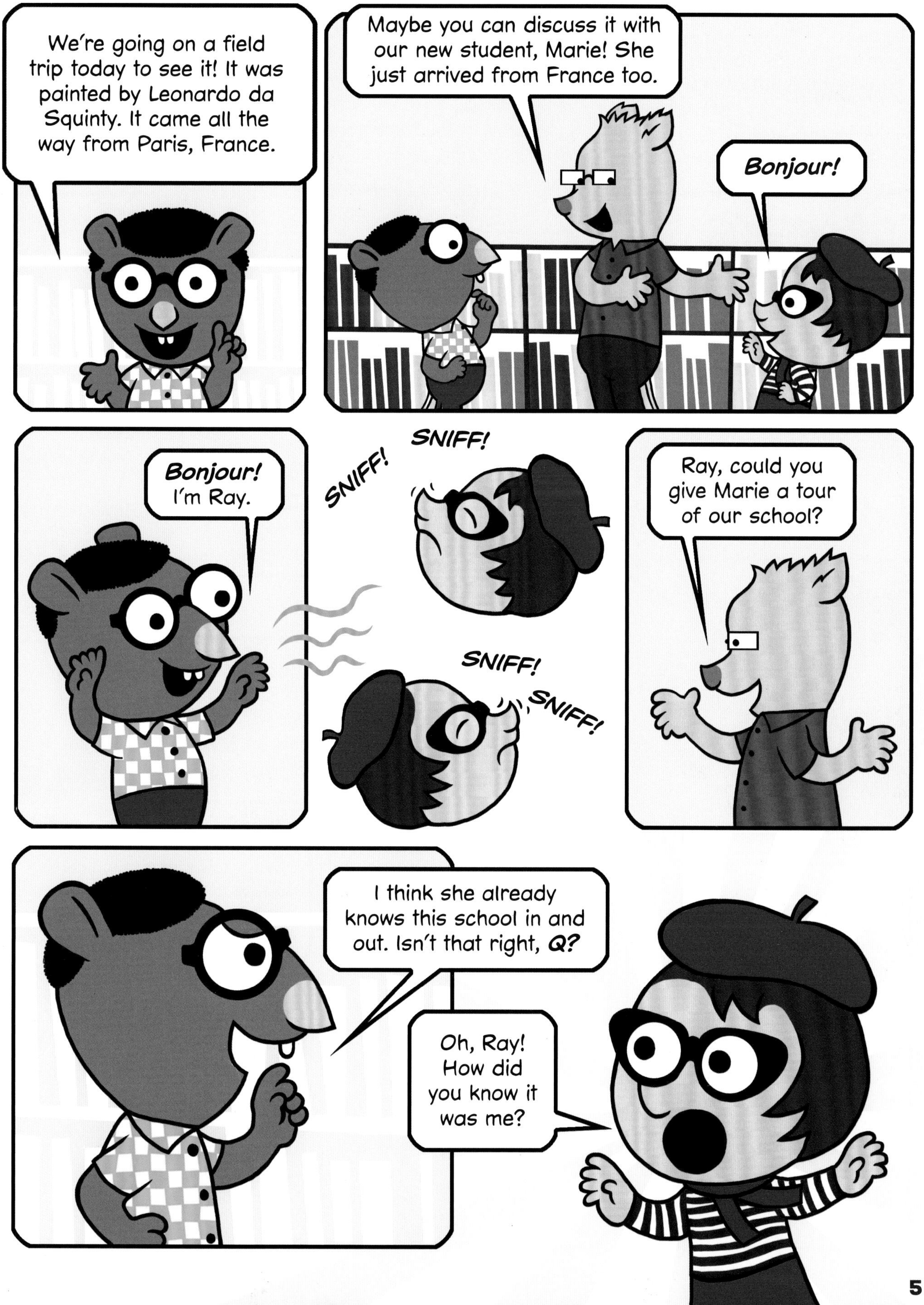

We're going on a field trip today to see it! It was painted by Leonardo da Squinty. It came all the way from Paris, France.
Maybe you can discuss it with our new student, Marie! She just arrived from France too.
Bonjour!
Bonjour! I'm Ray.
SNIFF!
SNIFF!
SNIFF!
SNIFF!
Ray, could you give Marie a tour of our school?
I think she already knows this school in and out. Isn't that right, Q?
Oh, Ray! How did you know it was me?

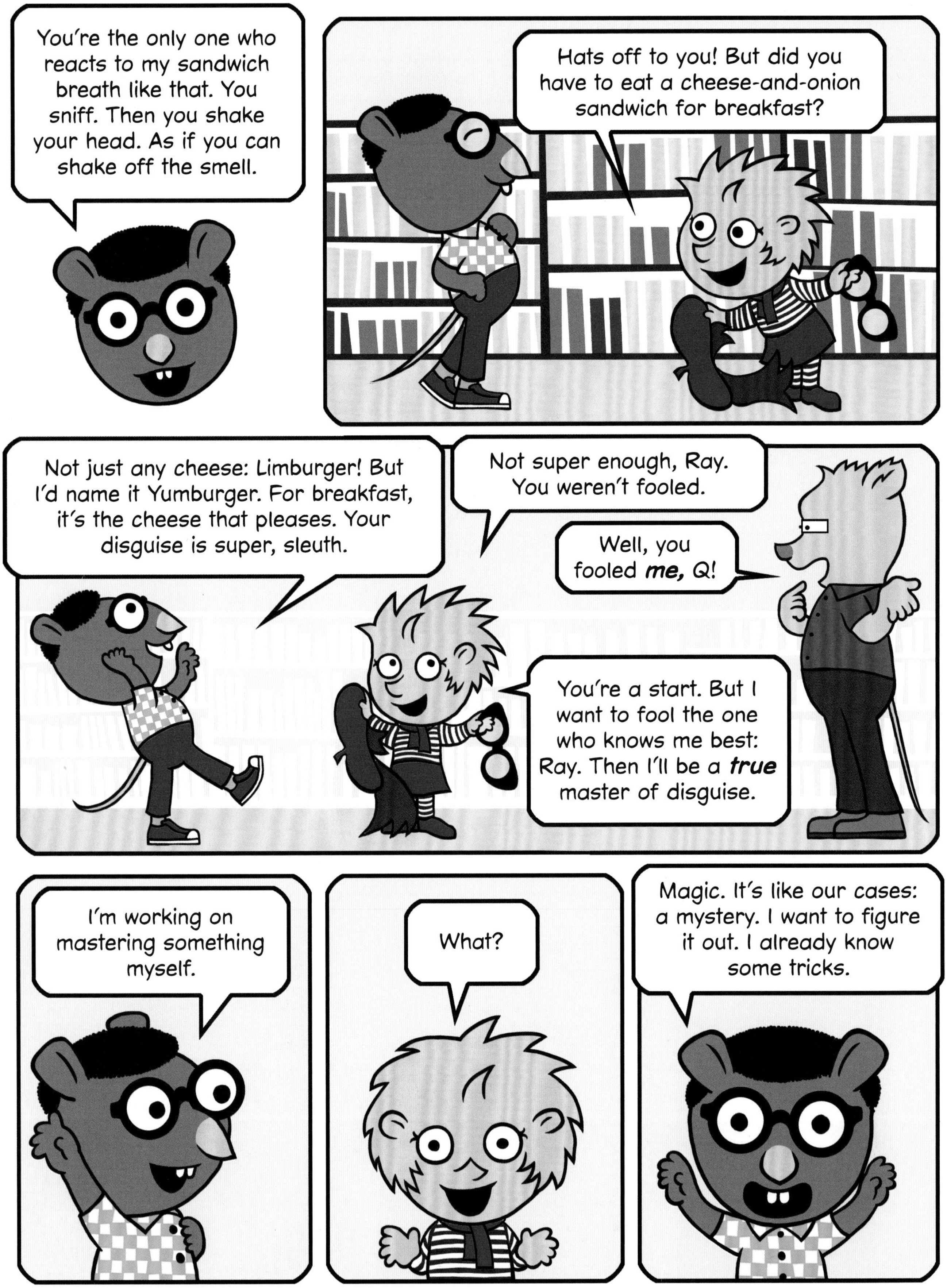
You're the only one who reacts to my sandwich breath like that. You sniff. Then you shake your head. As if you can shake off the smell.
Hats off to you! But did you have to eat a cheese-and-onion sandwich for breakfast?
Not just any cheese: Limburger! But I'd name it Yumburger. For breakfast, it's the cheese that pleases. Your disguise is super, sleuth.
Not super enough, Ray. You weren't fooled.
Well, you fooled ***me,*** Q!
You're a start. But I want to fool the one who knows me best: Ray. Then I'll be a ***true*** master of disguise.
I'm working on mastering something myself.
What?
Magic. It's like our cases: a mystery. I want to figure it out. I already know some tricks.

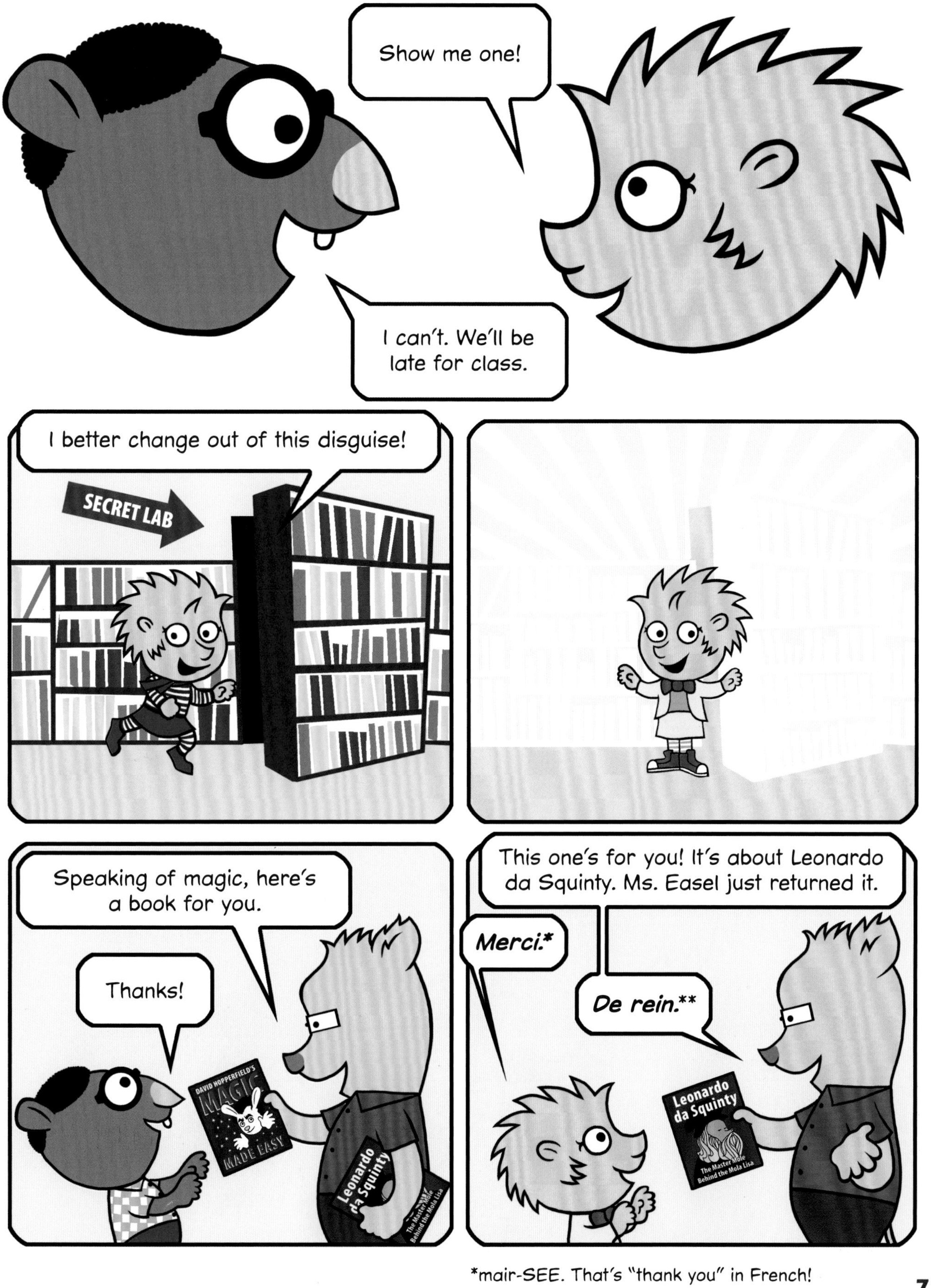
Show me one!
I can't. We'll be late for class.
SECRET LAB
I better change out of this disguise!
Speaking of magic, here's a book for you.
Thanks!
DAVID HOPPERFIELD'S MAGIC MADE EASY
Leonardo da Squinty
This one's for you! It's about Leonardo da Squinty. Ms. Easel just returned it.
Merci.*
De rein.**
Leonardo da Squinty The Master Mole Behind the Mola Lisa

*mair-SEE. That's "thank you" in French!
**duh-ree-ehn. That's "you're welcome"!

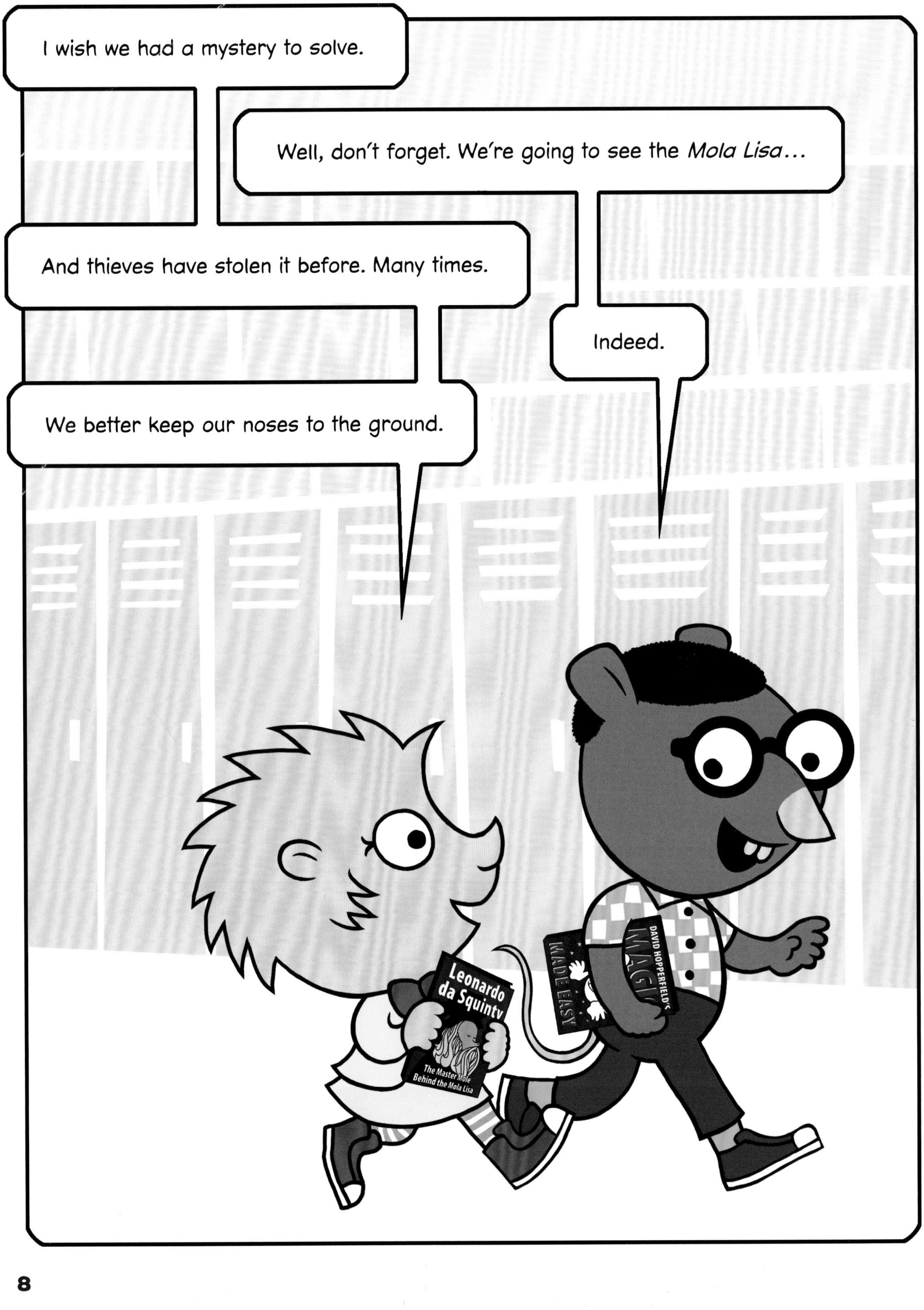
I wish we had a mystery to solve.
Well, don't forget. We're going to see the *Mola Lisa*...
And thieves have stolen it before. Many times.
Indeed.
We better keep our noses to the ground.
Leonardo da Squinty
The Master Mole Behind the Mola Lisa
DAVID HOPPERFIELD'S
MADE EASY

CHAPTER TWO
The Magic Show

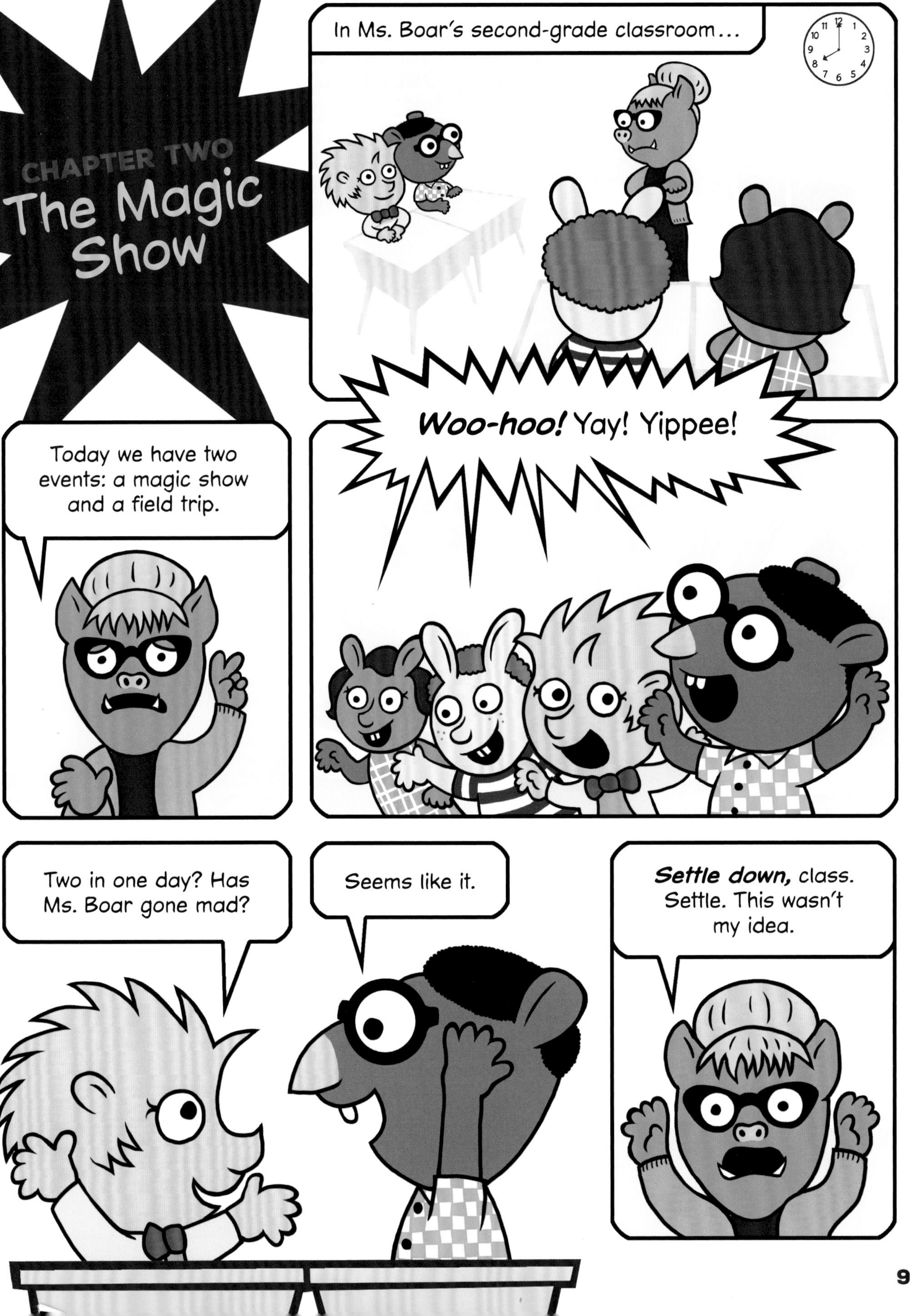

In Ms. Boar's second-grade classroom...
Today we have two events: a magic show and a field trip.
Woo-hoo! Yay! Yippee!
Two in one day? Has Ms. Boar gone mad?
Seems like it.
Settle down, class. Settle. This wasn't my idea.

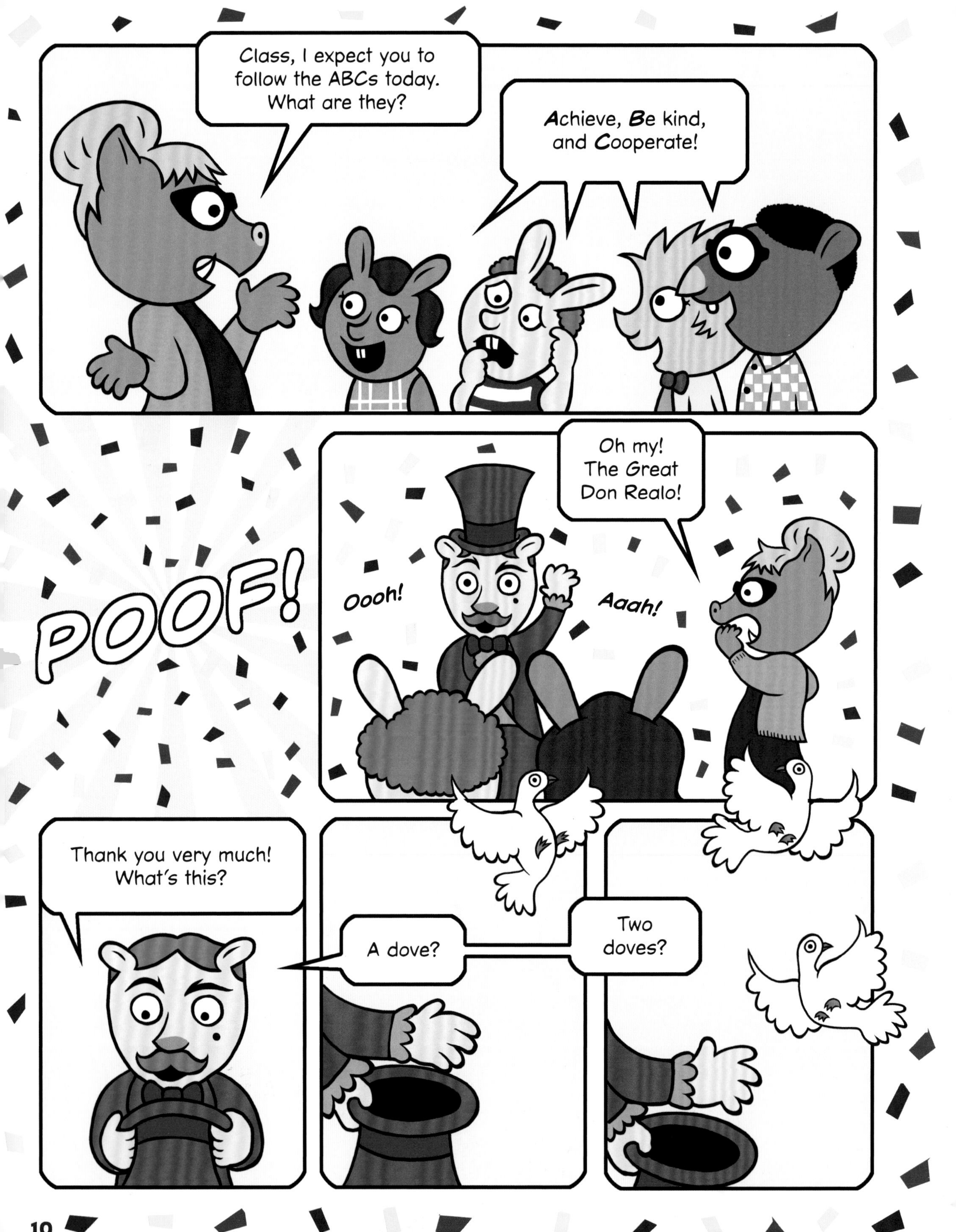
Class, I expect you to follow the ABCs today. What are they?
Achieve, Be kind, and Cooperate!
POOF!
Oooh!
Aaah!
Oh my! The Great Don Realo!
Thank you very much! What's this?
A dove?
Two doves?

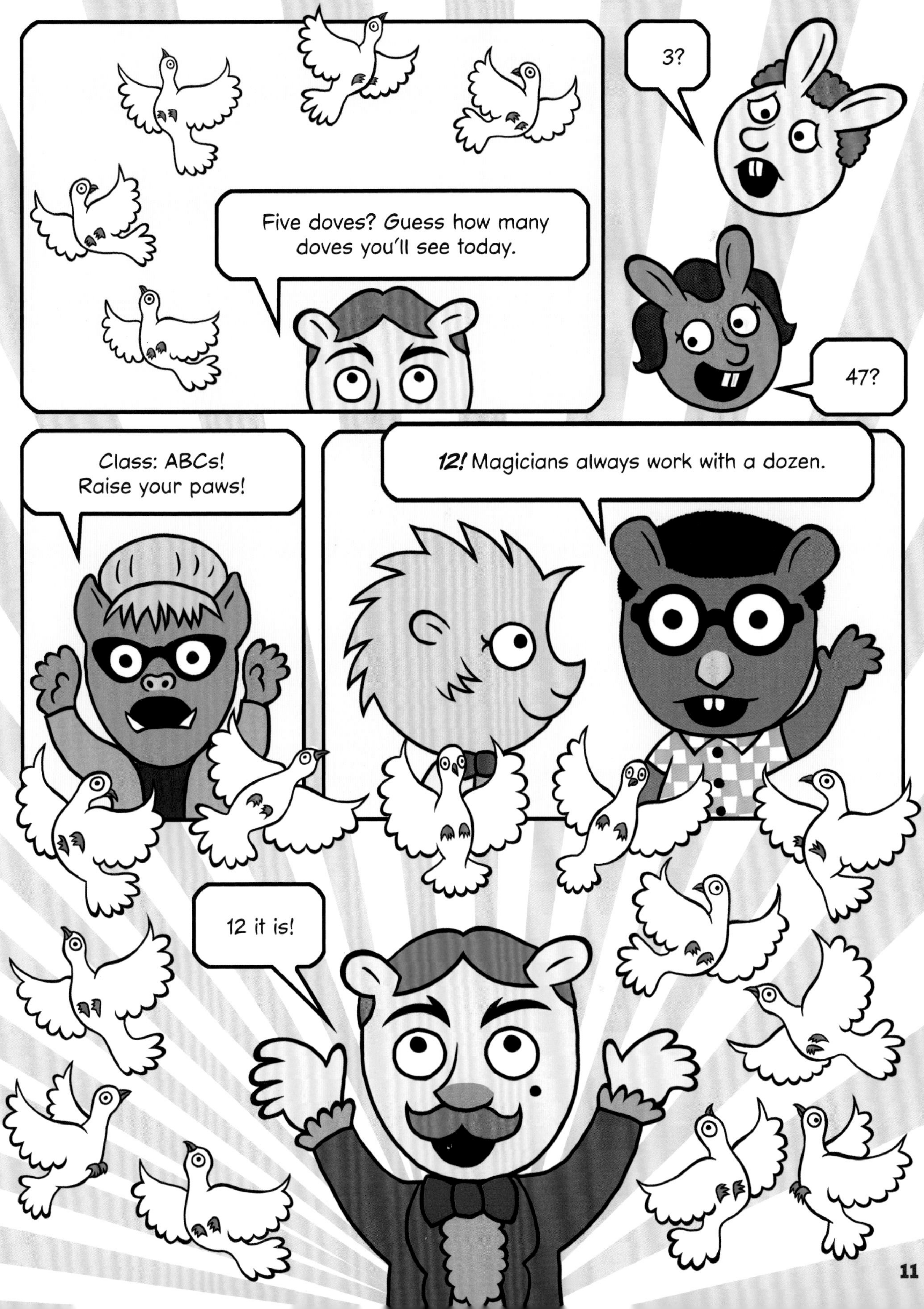
Five doves? Guess how many doves you'll see today.
3?
47?
Class: ABCs! Raise your paws!
12! Magicians always work with a dozen.
12 it is!

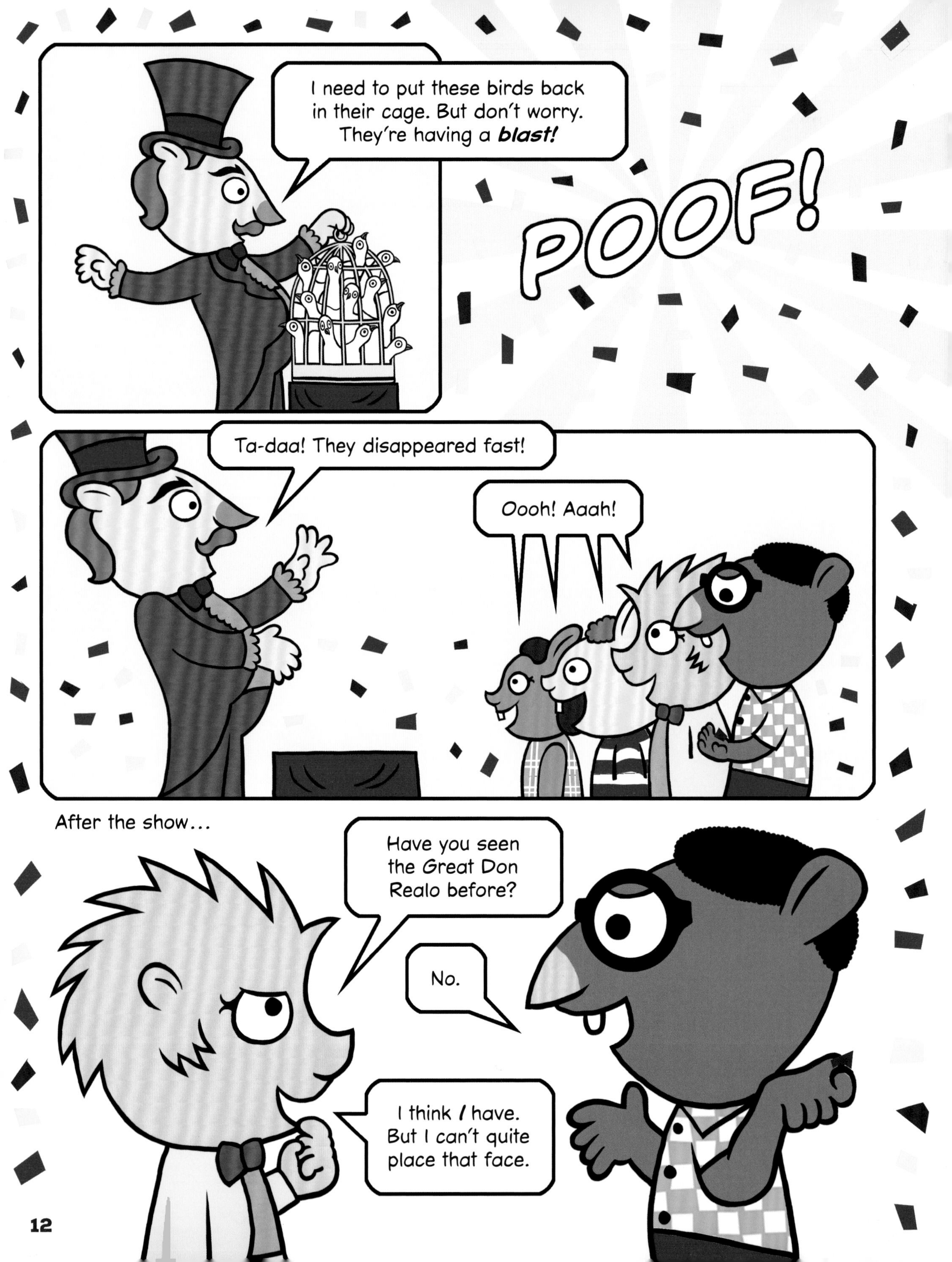
I need to put these birds back in their cage. But don't worry. They're having a ***blast!***
POOF!
Ta-daa! They disappeared fast!
Oooh! Aaah!
After the show...
Have you seen the Great Don Realo before?
No.
I think *I* have. But I can't quite place that face.

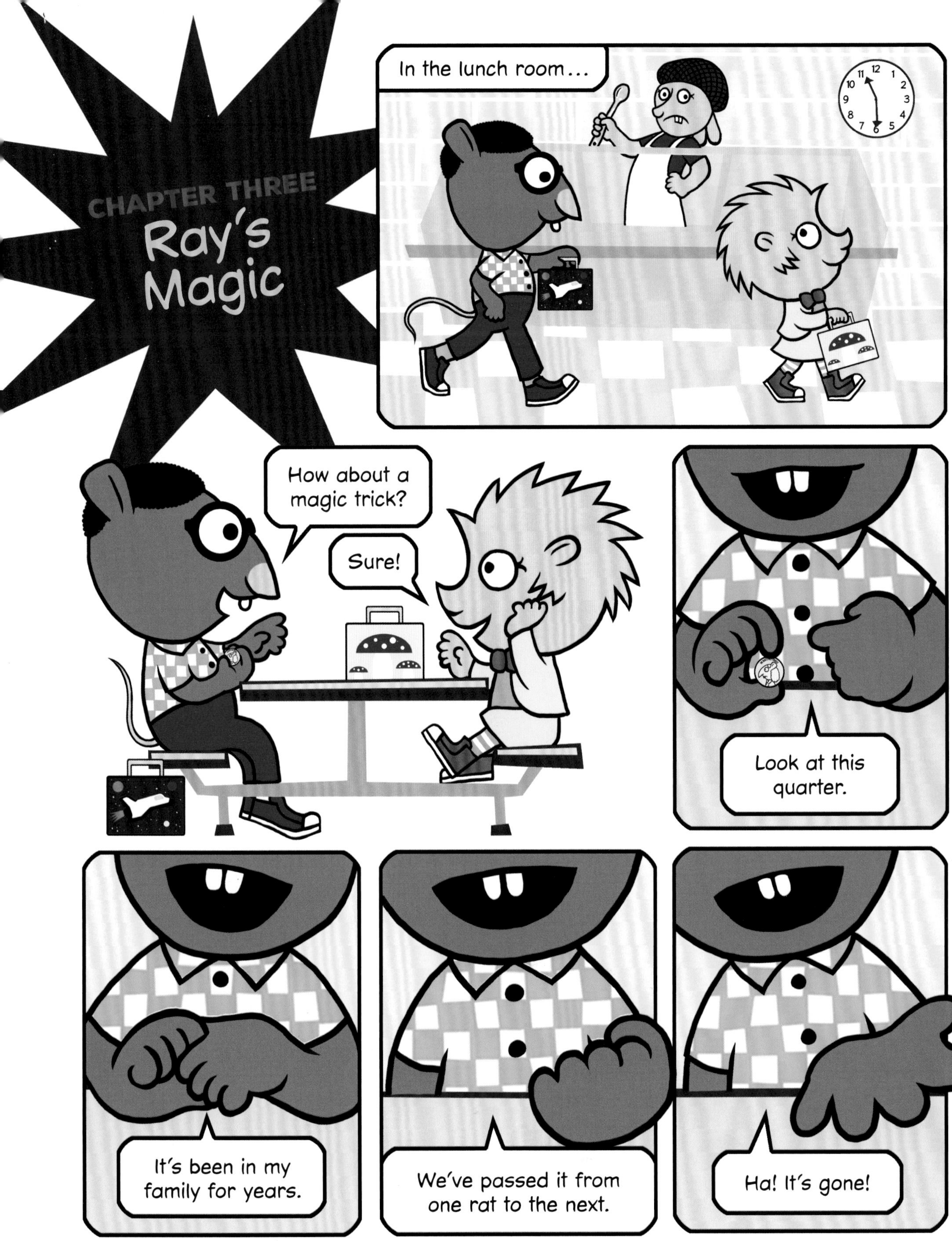
CHAPTER THREE
Ray's Magic
In the lunch room...
How about a magic trick?
Sure!
Look at this quarter.
It's been in my family for years.
We've passed it from one rat to the next.
Ha! It's gone!

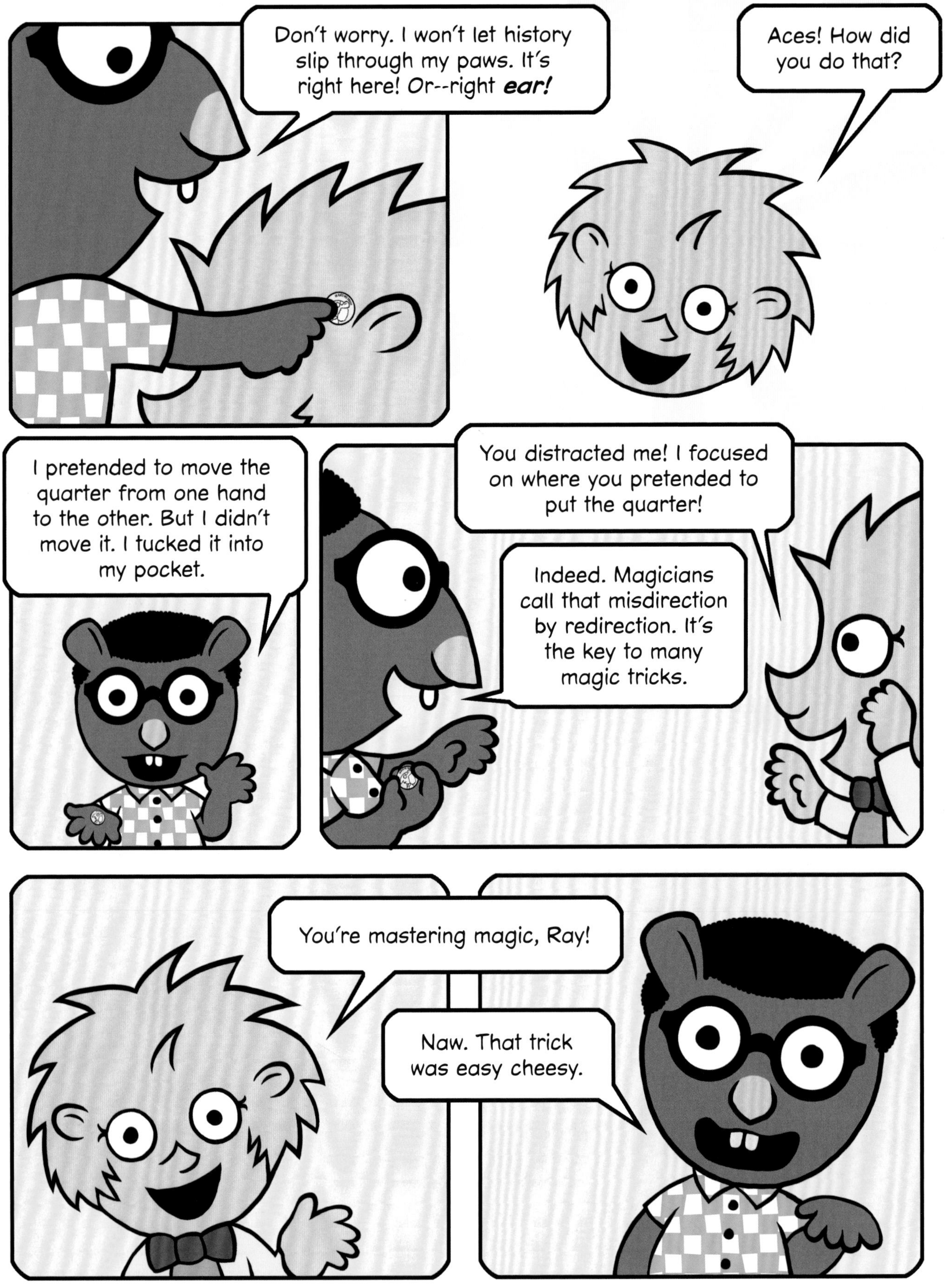
Don't worry. I won't let history slip through my paws. It's right here! Or--right ***ear!***
Aces! How did you do that?
I pretended to move the quarter from one hand to the other. But I didn't move it. I tucked it into my pocket.
You distracted me! I focused on where you pretended to put the quarter!
Indeed. Magicians call that misdirection by redirection. It's the key to many magic tricks.
You're mastering magic, Ray!
Naw. That trick was easy cheesy.

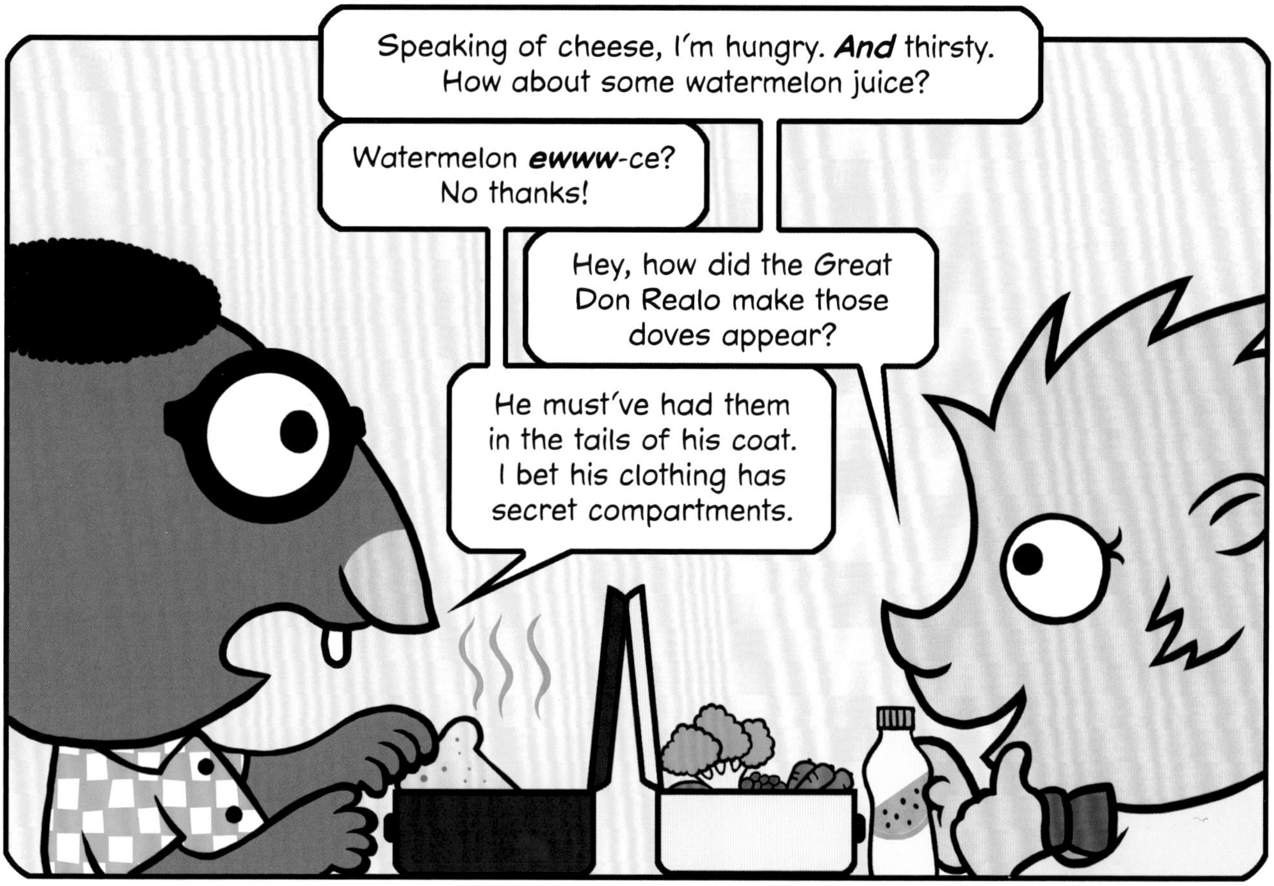
Speaking of cheese, I'm hungry. ***And*** thirsty. How about some watermelon juice?
Watermelon ***ewww***-ce? No thanks!
Hey, how did the Great Don Realo make those doves appear?
He must've had them in the tails of his coat. I bet his clothing has secret compartments.

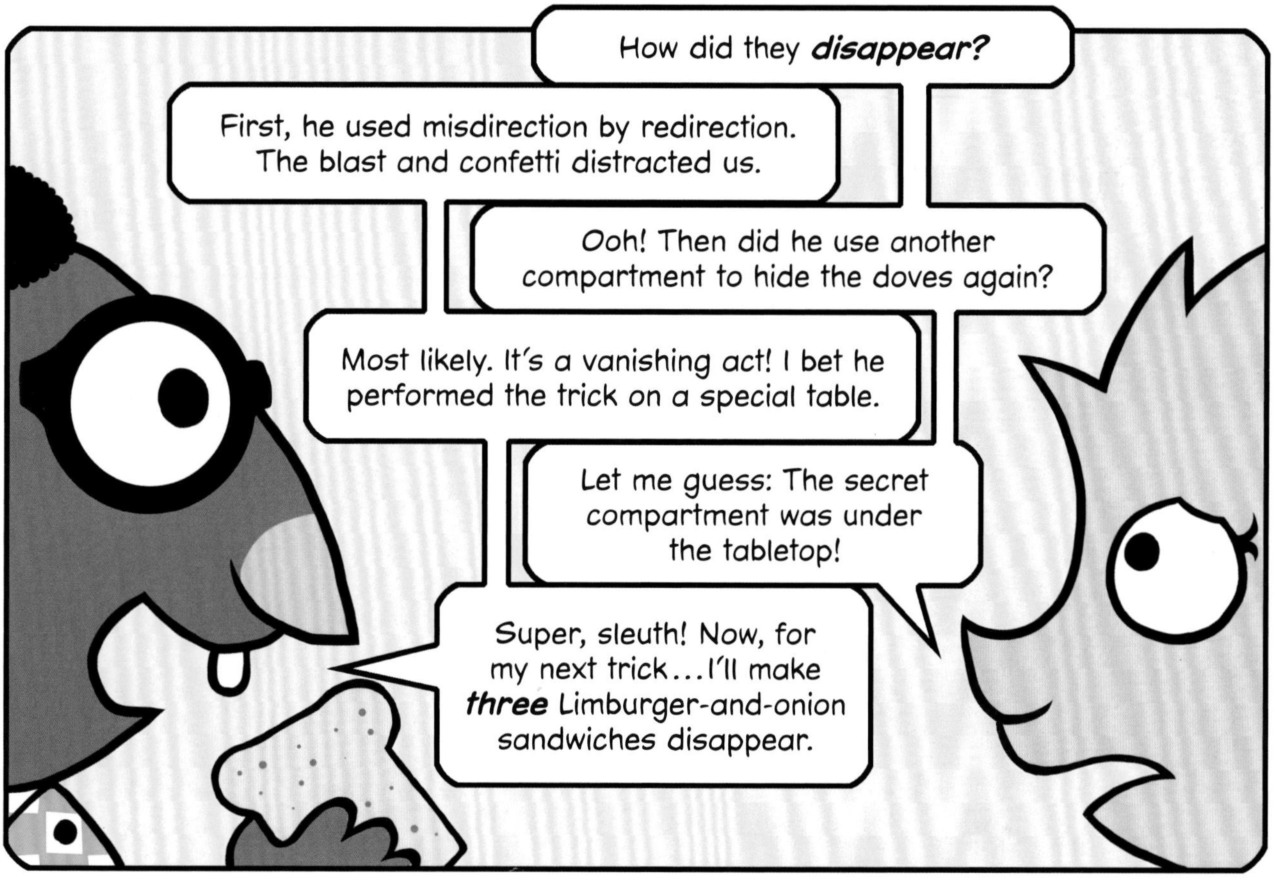
How did they ***disappear?***
First, he used misdirection by redirection. The blast and confetti distracted us.
Ooh! Then did he use another compartment to hide the doves again?
Most likely. It's a vanishing act! I bet he performed the trick on a special table.
Let me guess: The secret compartment was under the tabletop!
Super, sleuth! Now, for my next trick...I'll make ***three*** Limburger-and-onion sandwiches disappear.

CHAPTER FOUR
The Mola Lisa is Missing!

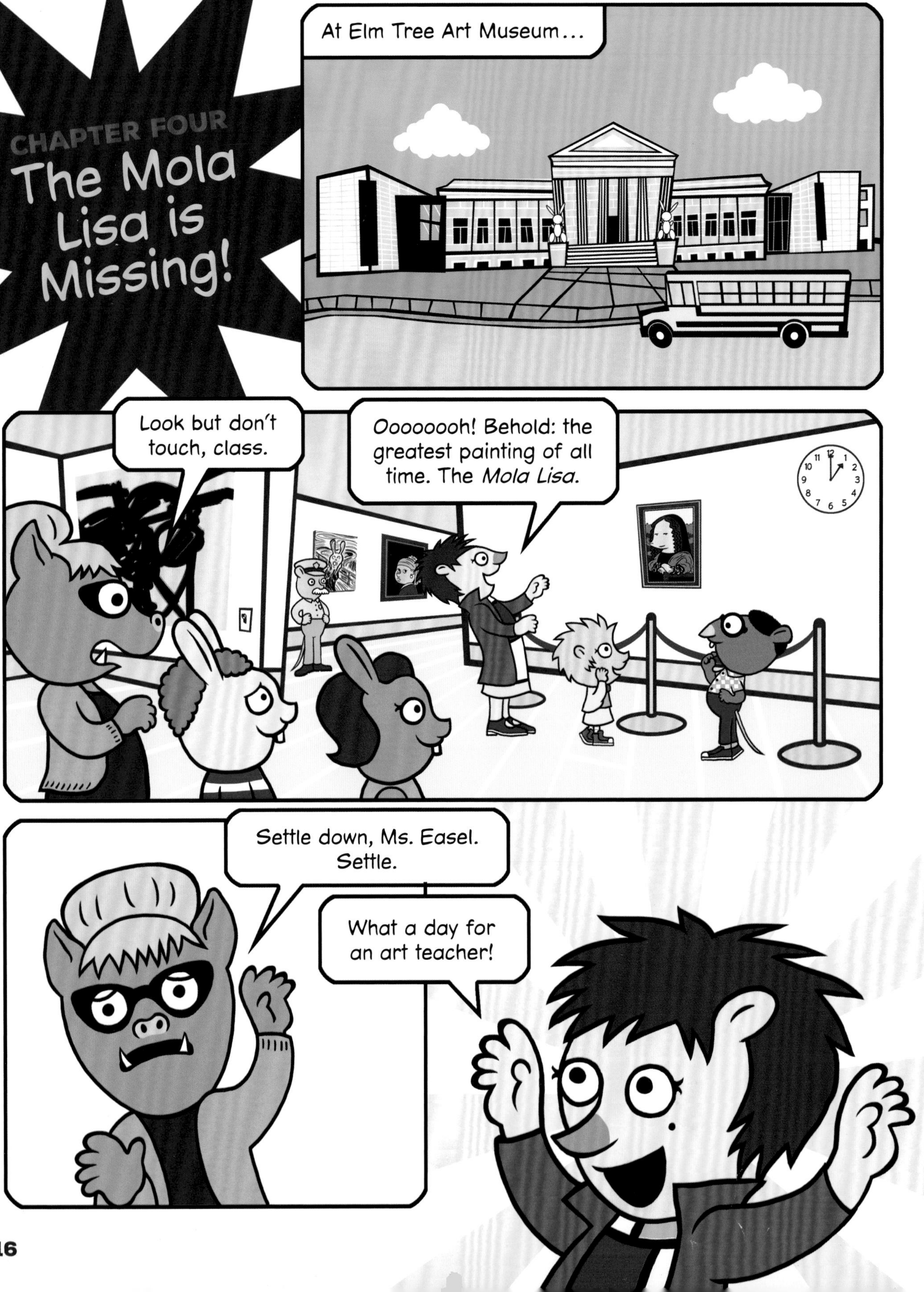

At Elm Tree Art Museum...
Look but don't touch, class.
Ooooooh! Behold: the greatest painting of all time. The *Mola Lisa*.
Settle down, Ms. Easel. Settle.
What a day for an art teacher!

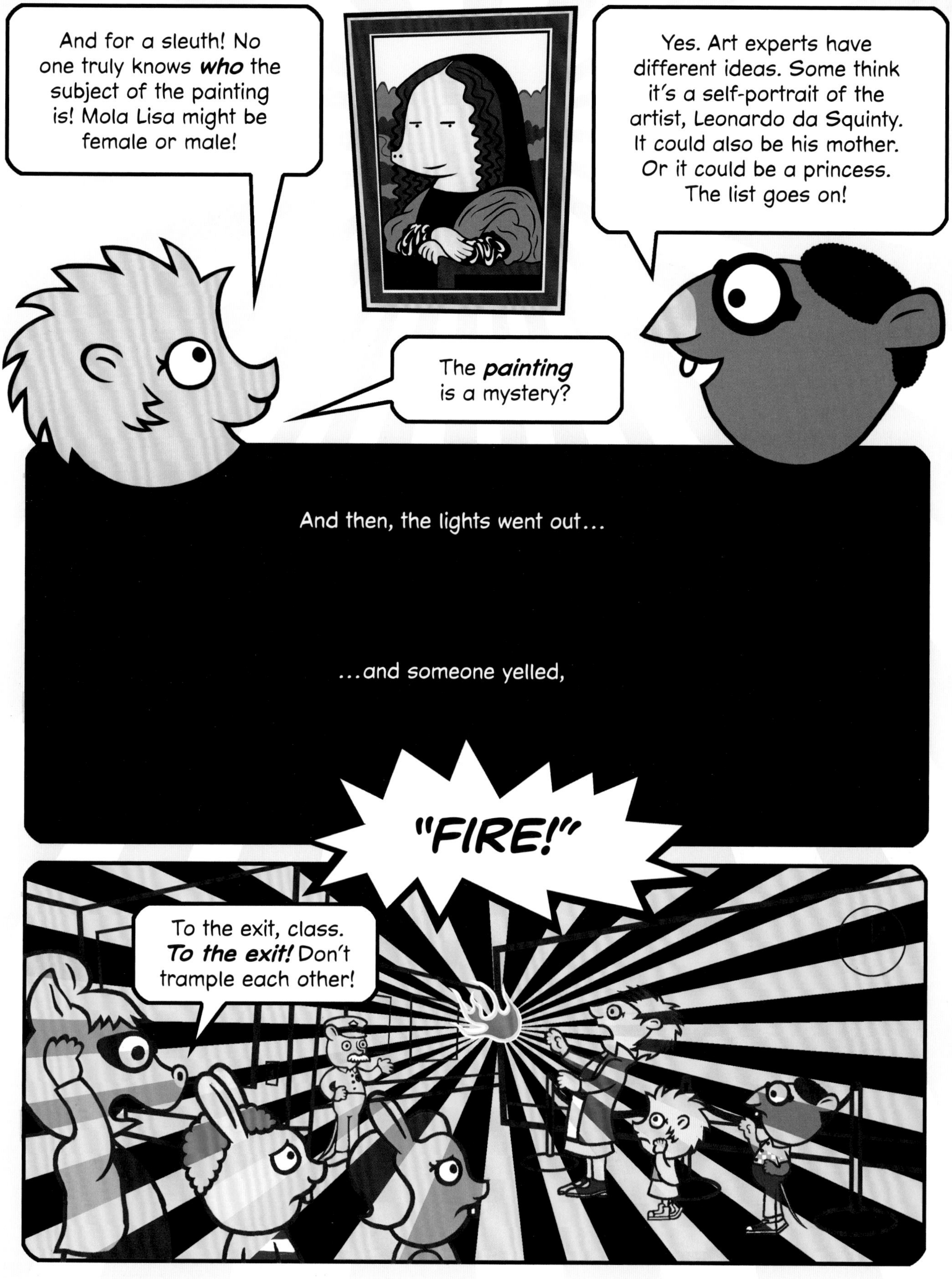
And for a sleuth! No one truly knows ***who*** the subject of the painting is! Mola Lisa might be female or male!
Yes. Art experts have different ideas. Some think it's a self-portrait of the artist, Leonardo da Squinty. It could also be his mother. Or it could be a princess. The list goes on!
The ***painting*** is a mystery?
And then, the lights went out...
...and someone yelled,
"FIRE!"
To the exit, class. ***To the exit!*** Don't trample each other!

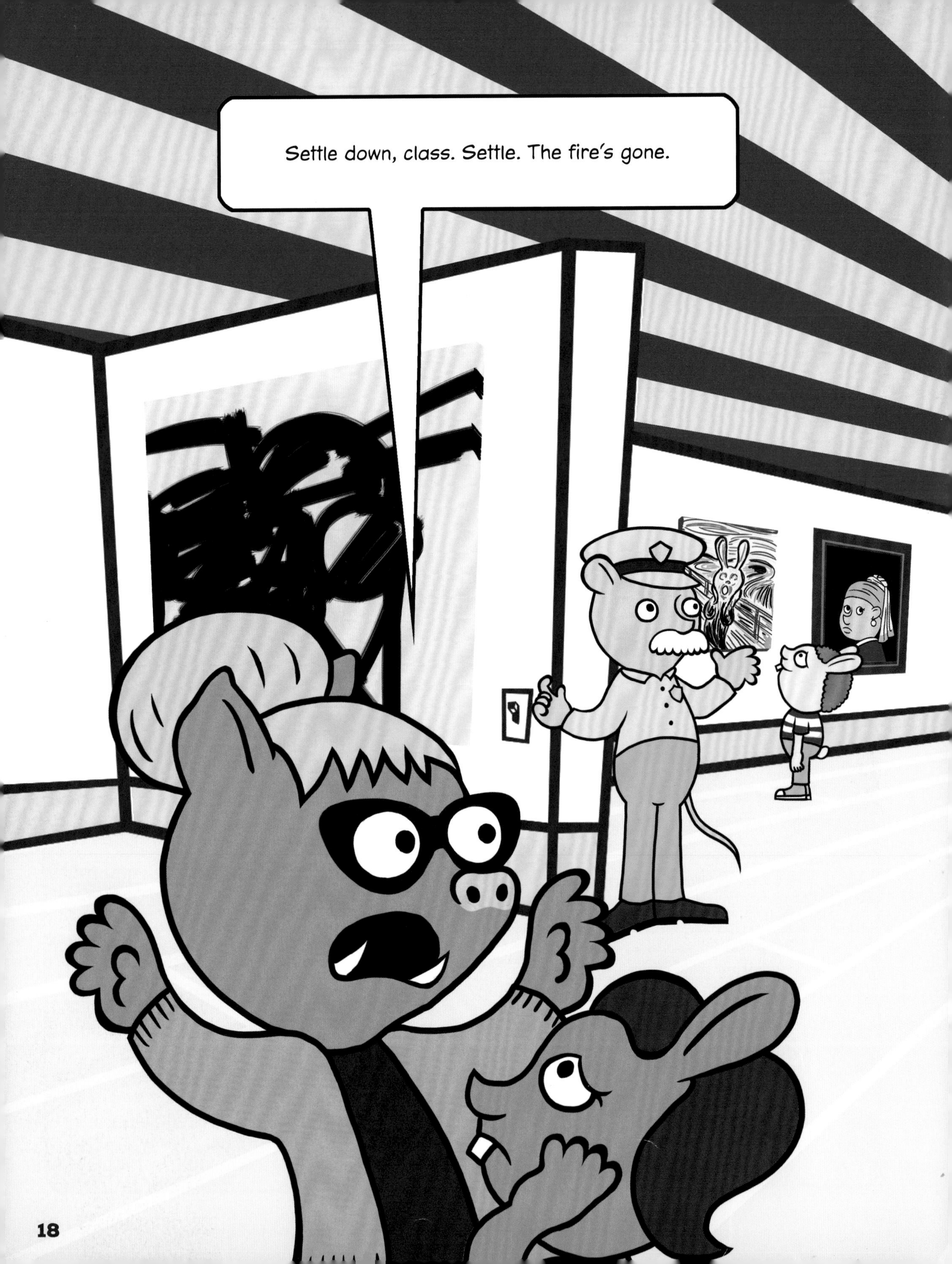
Settle down, class. Settle. The fire's gone.

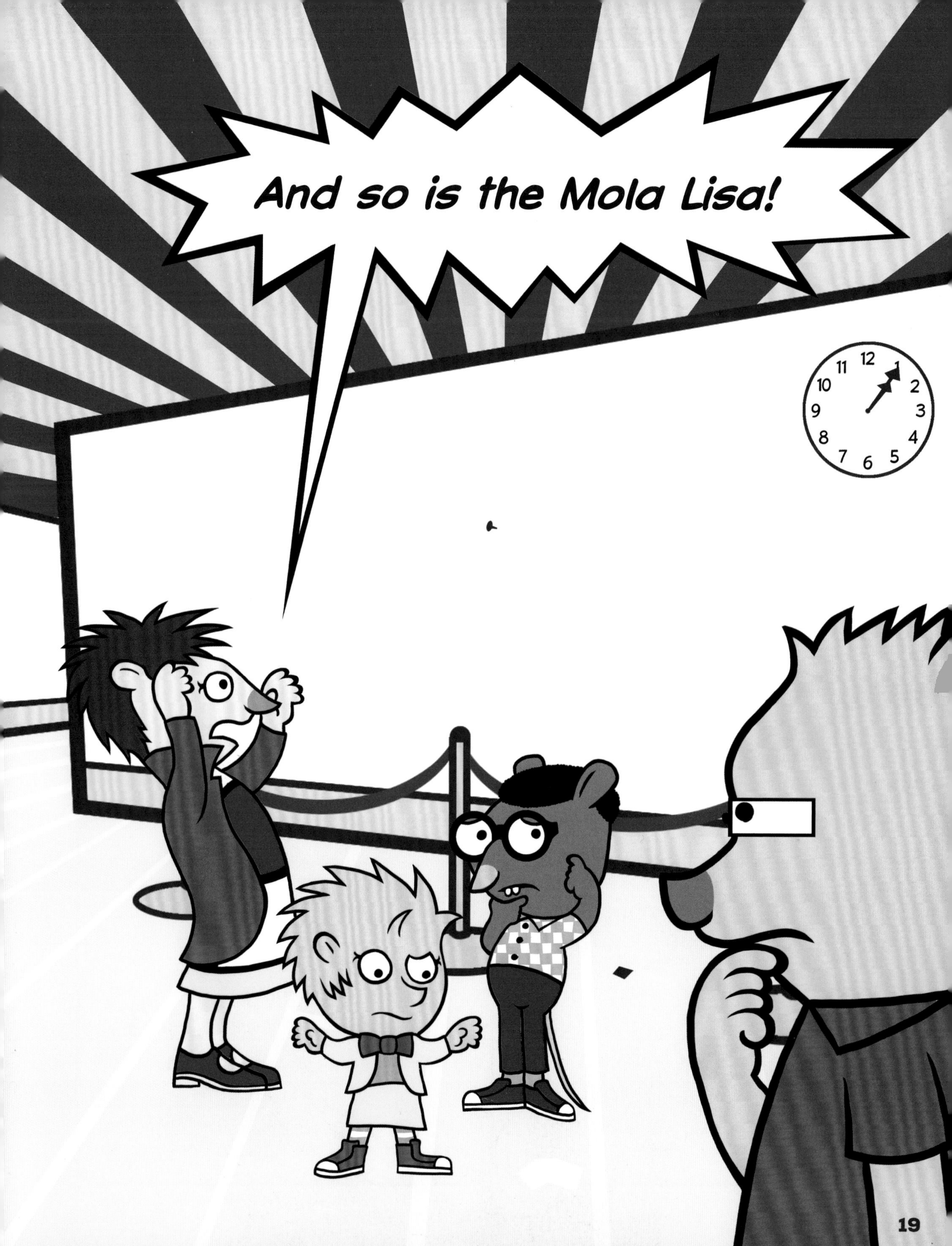
And so is the Mola Lisa!

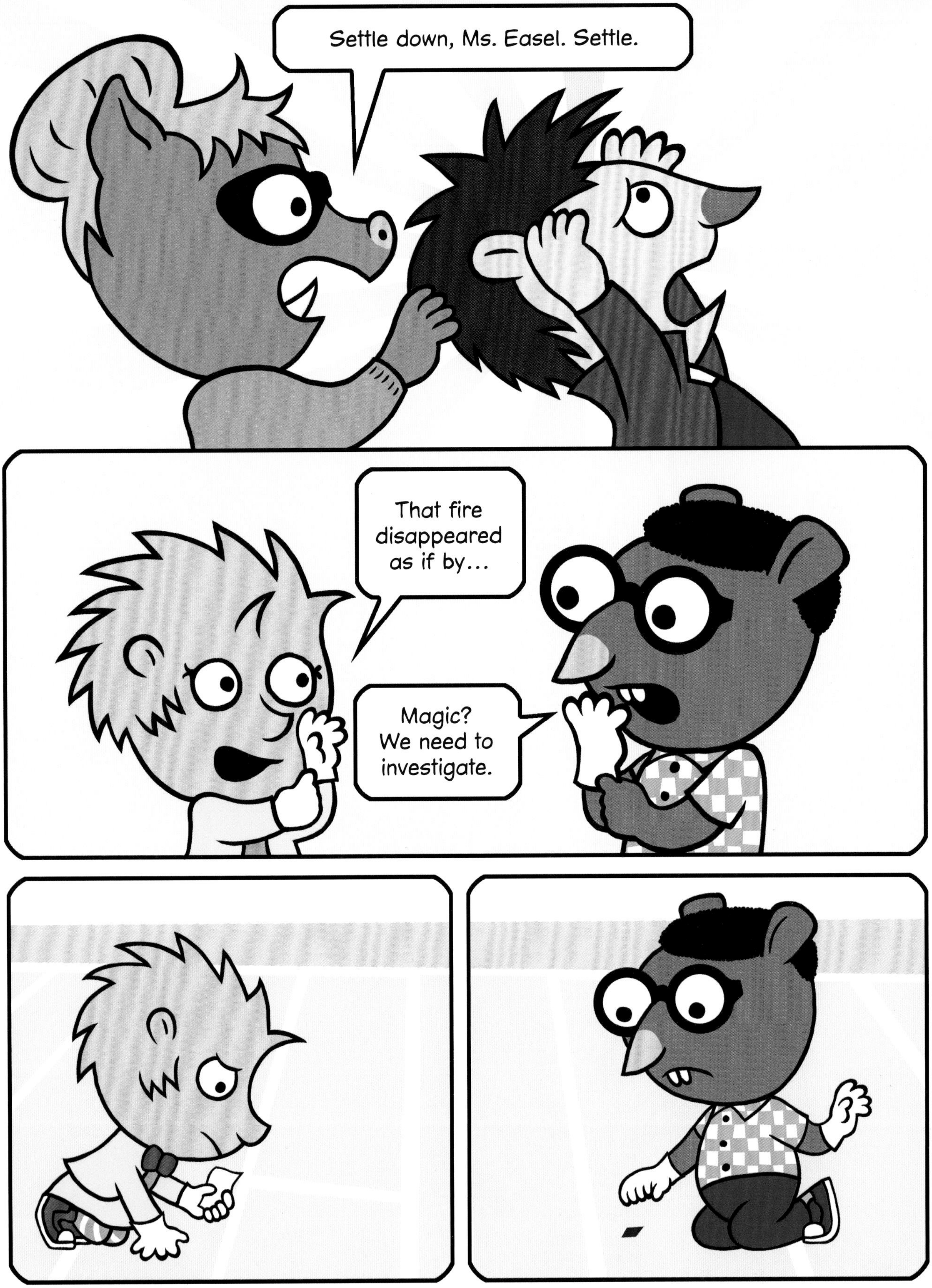
Settle down, Ms. Easel. Settle.
That fire disappeared as if by...
Magic? We need to investigate.

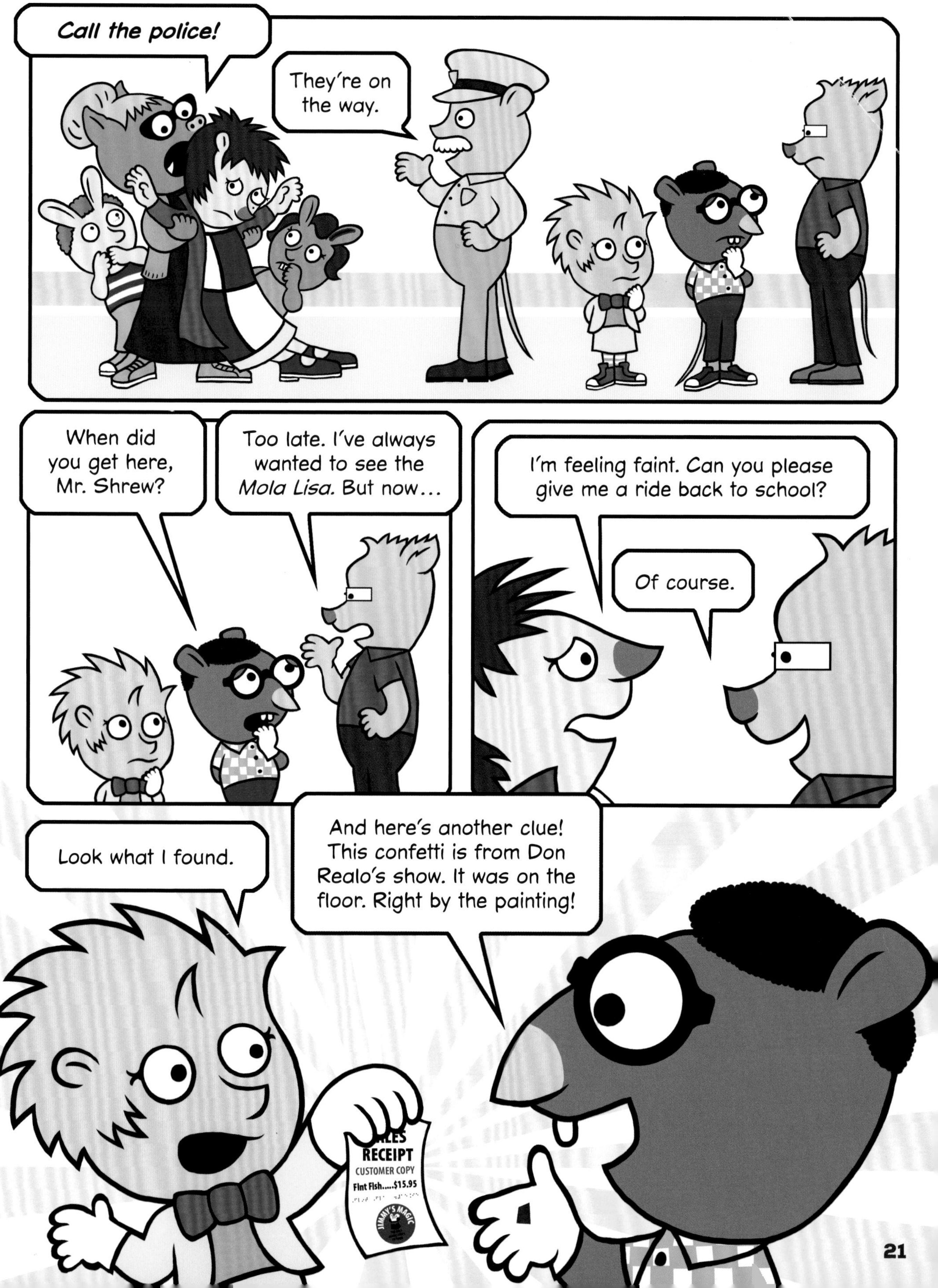
Call the police!
They're on the way.
When did you get here, Mr. Shrew?
Too late. I've always wanted to see the *Mola Lisa.* But now...
I'm feeling faint. Can you please give me a ride back to school?
Of course.
Look what I found.
RECEIPT
CUSTOMER COPY
Fint Fish.....$15.95
JIMMY'S MAGIC
And here's another clue! This confetti is from Don Realo's show. It was on the floor. Right by the painting!

CHAPTER FIVE

Following the Clues...

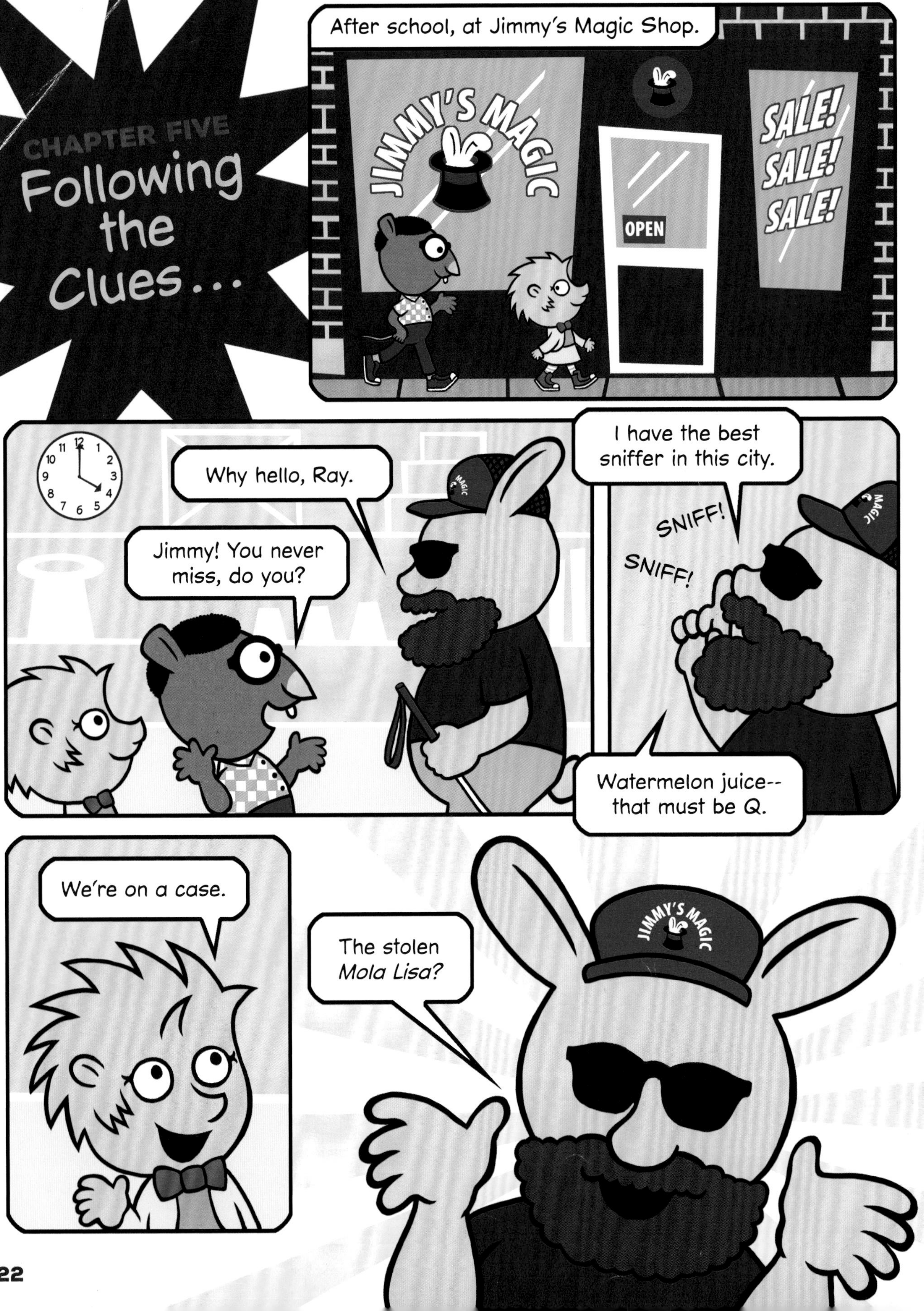

After school, at Jimmy's Magic Shop.
JIMMY'S MAGIC
OPEN
SALE! SALE! SALE!
Why hello, Ray.
Jimmy! You never miss, do you?
MAGIC
I have the best sniffer in this city.
SNIFF!
SNIFF!
Watermelon juice--that must be Q.
We're on a case.
The stolen *Mola Lisa?*
JIMMY'S MAGIC

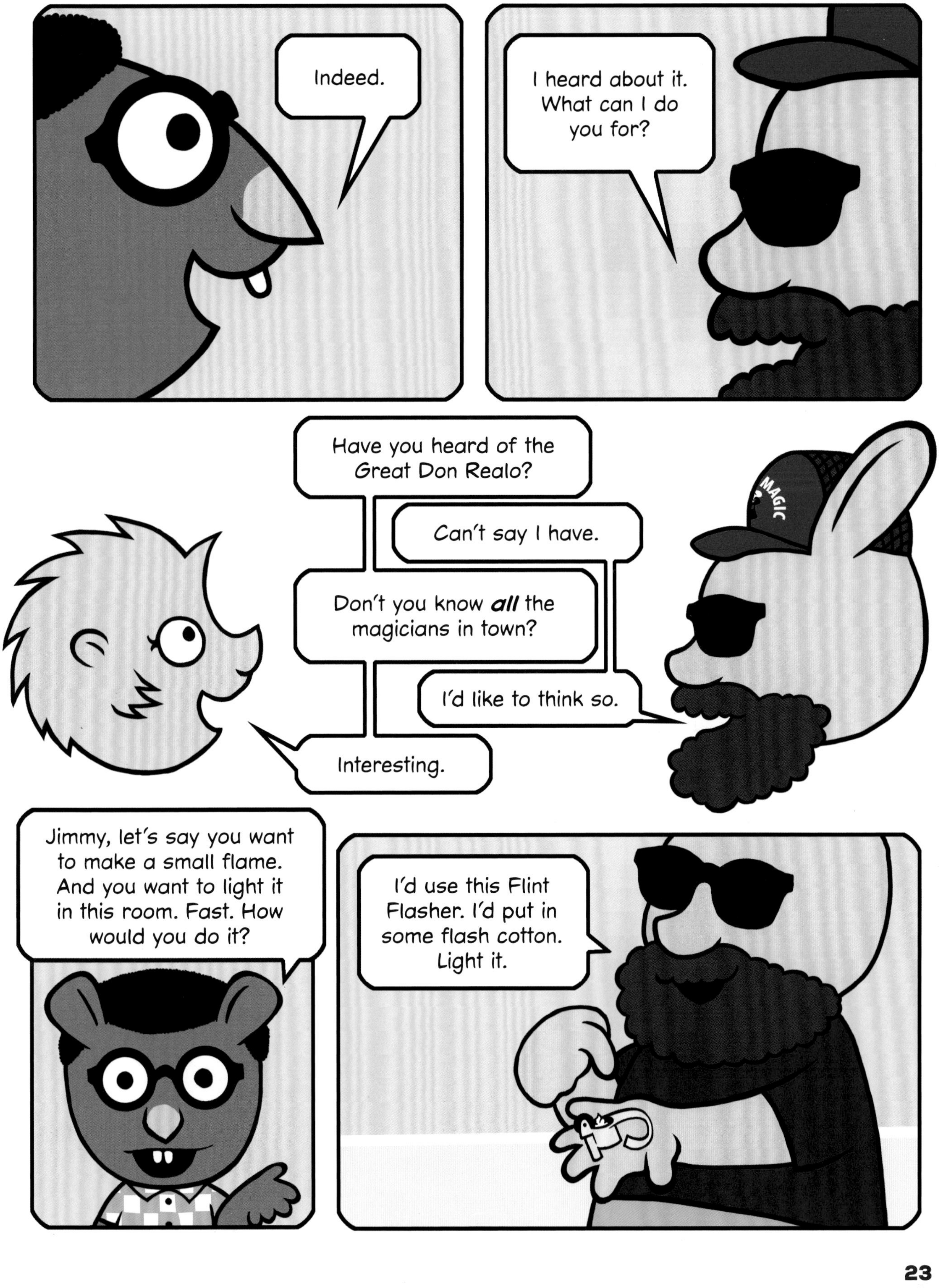
Indeed.
I heard about it. What can I do you for?
Have you heard of the Great Don Realo?
Can't say I have.
MAGIC
Don't you know ***all*** the magicians in town?
I'd like to think so.
Interesting.
Jimmy, let's say you want to make a small flame. And you want to light it in this room. Fast. How would you do it?
I'd use this Flint Flasher. I'd put in some flash cotton. Light it.

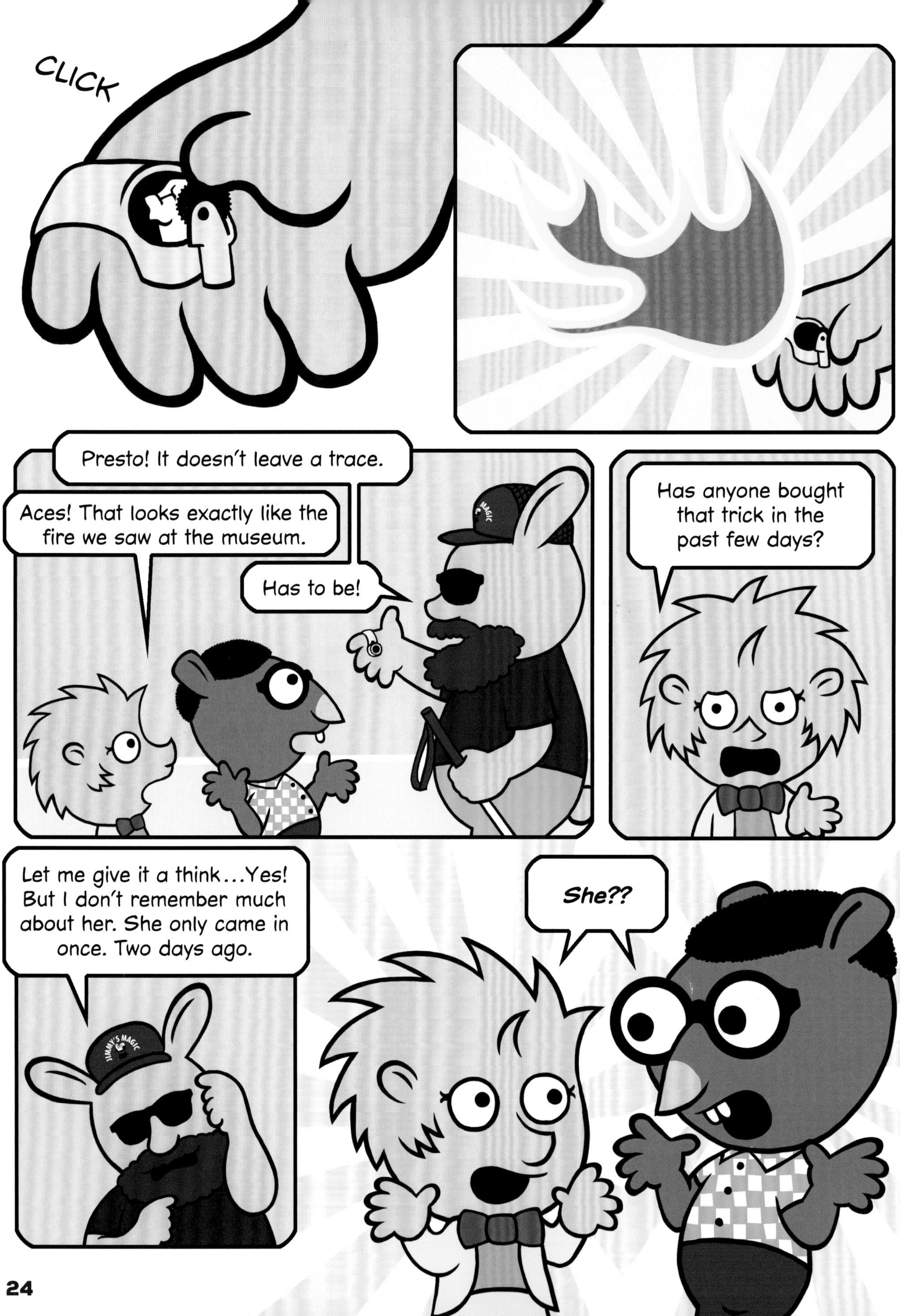
CLICK
Presto! It doesn't leave a trace.
Aces! That looks exactly like the fire we saw at the museum.
Has to be!
MAGIC
Has anyone bought that trick in the past few days?
Let me give it a think...Yes! But I don't remember much about her. She only came in once. Two days ago.
JIMMY'S MAGIC
She??

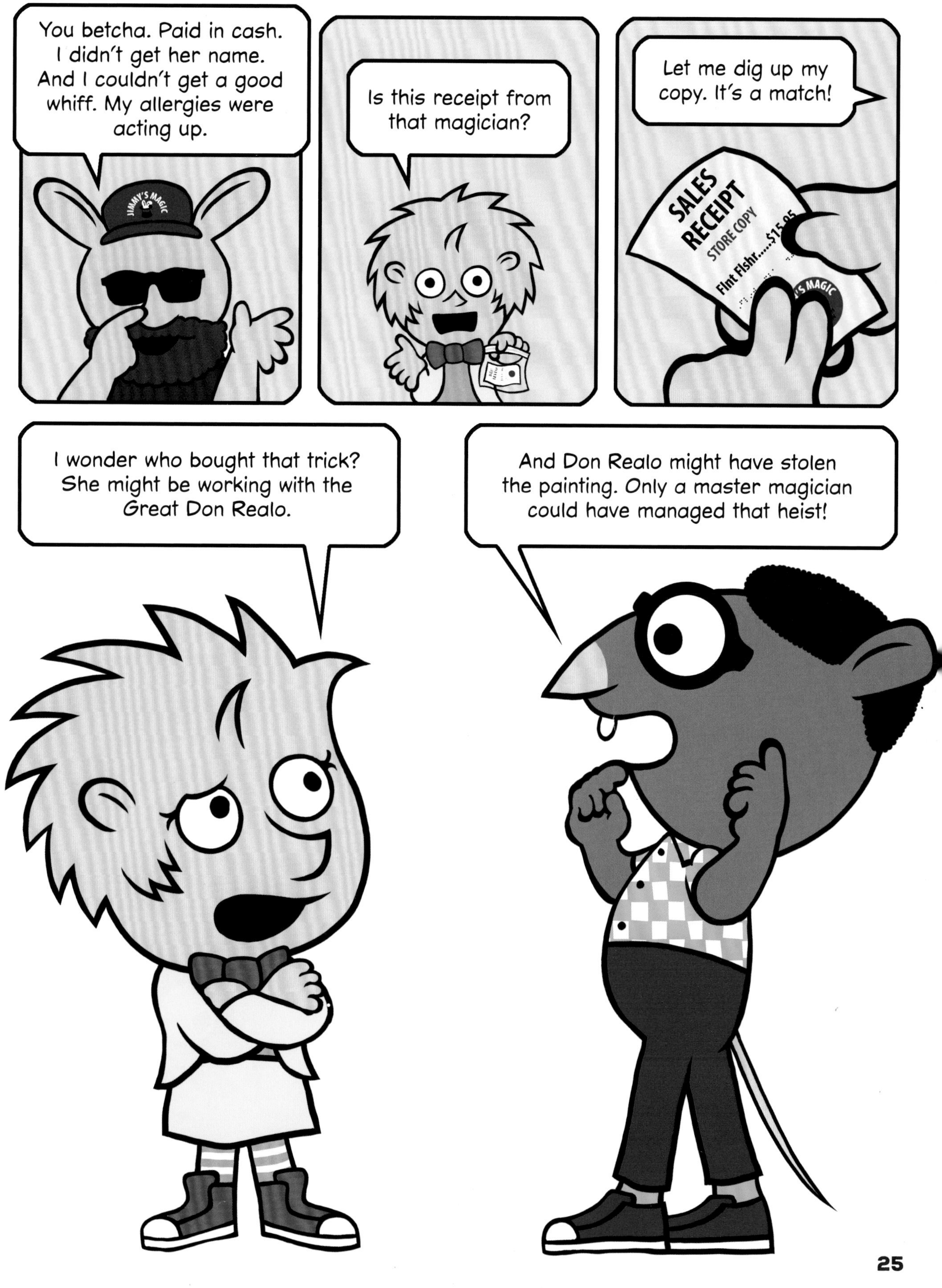
You betcha. Paid in cash. I didn't get her name. And I couldn't get a good whiff. My allergies were acting up.
JIMMY'S MAGIC
Is this receipt from that magician?
Let me dig up my copy. It's a match!
SALES RECEIPT
STORE COPY
I wonder who bought that trick? She might be working with the Great Don Realo.
And Don Realo might have stolen the painting. Only a master magician could have managed that heist!

CHAPTER SIX

Searching for Suspects

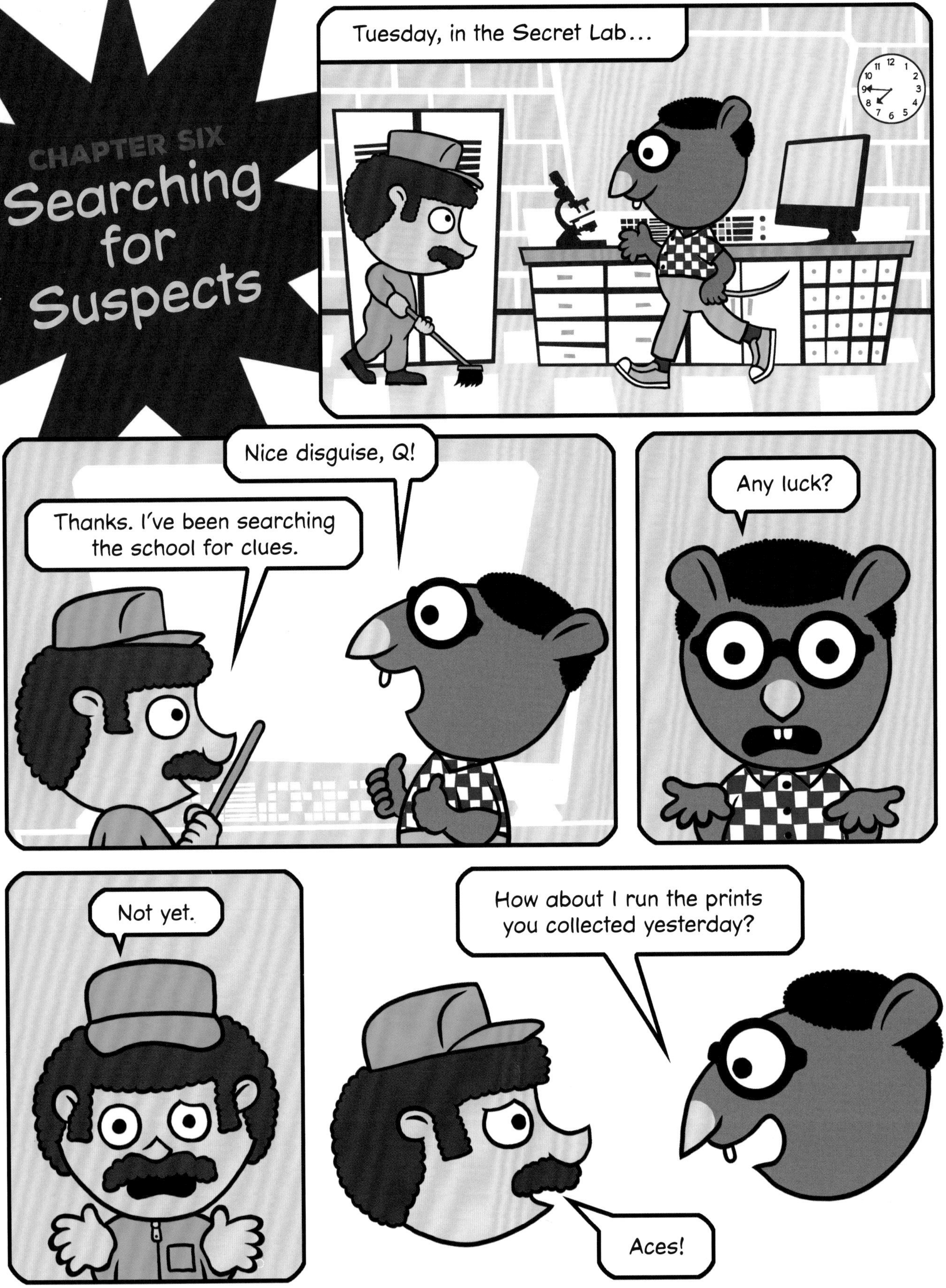

Tuesday, in the Secret Lab...
Nice disguise, Q!
Thanks. I've been searching the school for clues.
Any luck?
Not yet.
How about I run the prints you collected yesterday?
Aces!

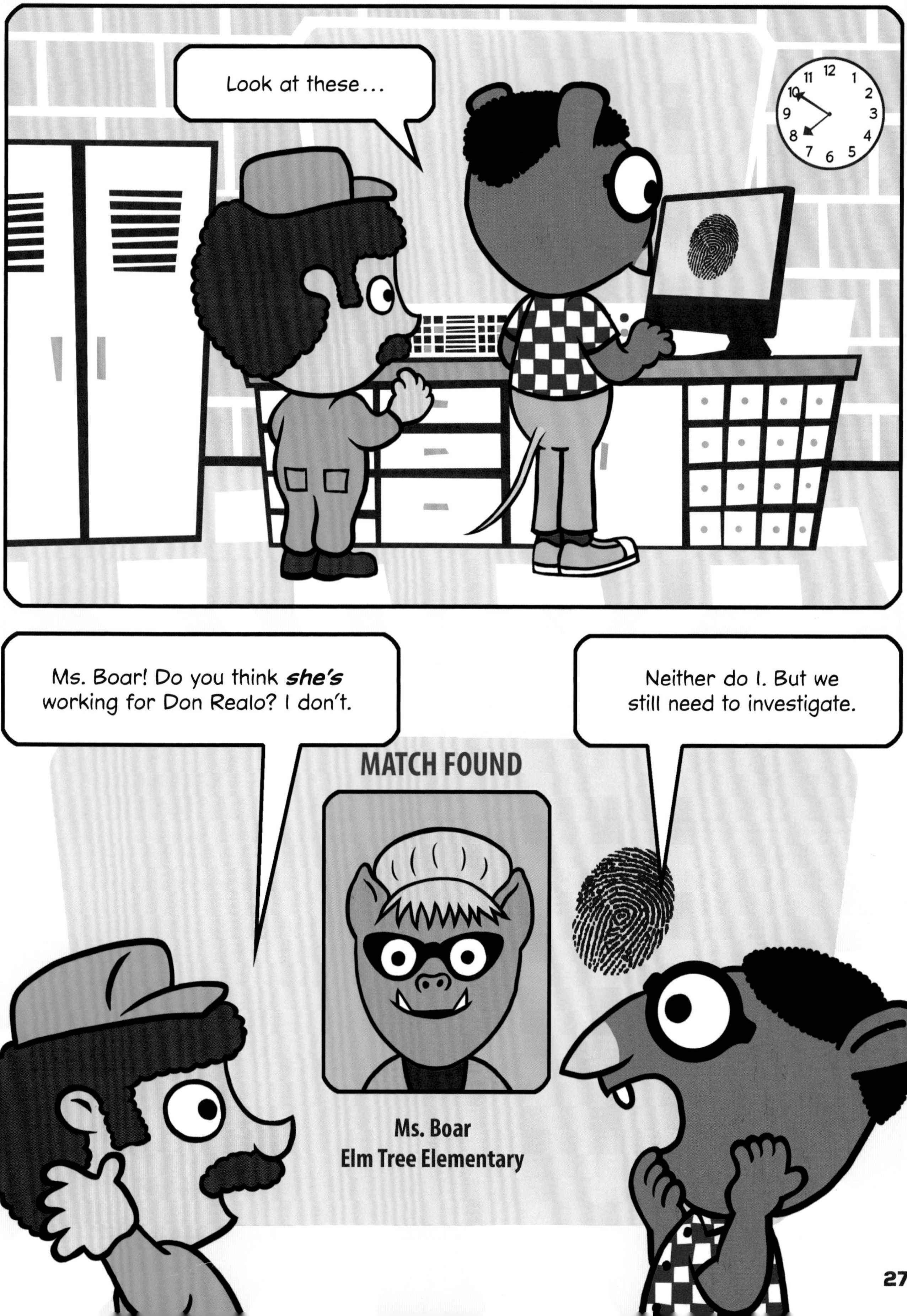

Look at these...
11 12 1 2 3 4 5 6 7 8 9 10
Ms. Boar! Do you think ***she's*** working for Don Realo? I don't.
Neither do I. But we still need to investigate.
MATCH FOUND
Ms. Boar
Elm Tree Elementary

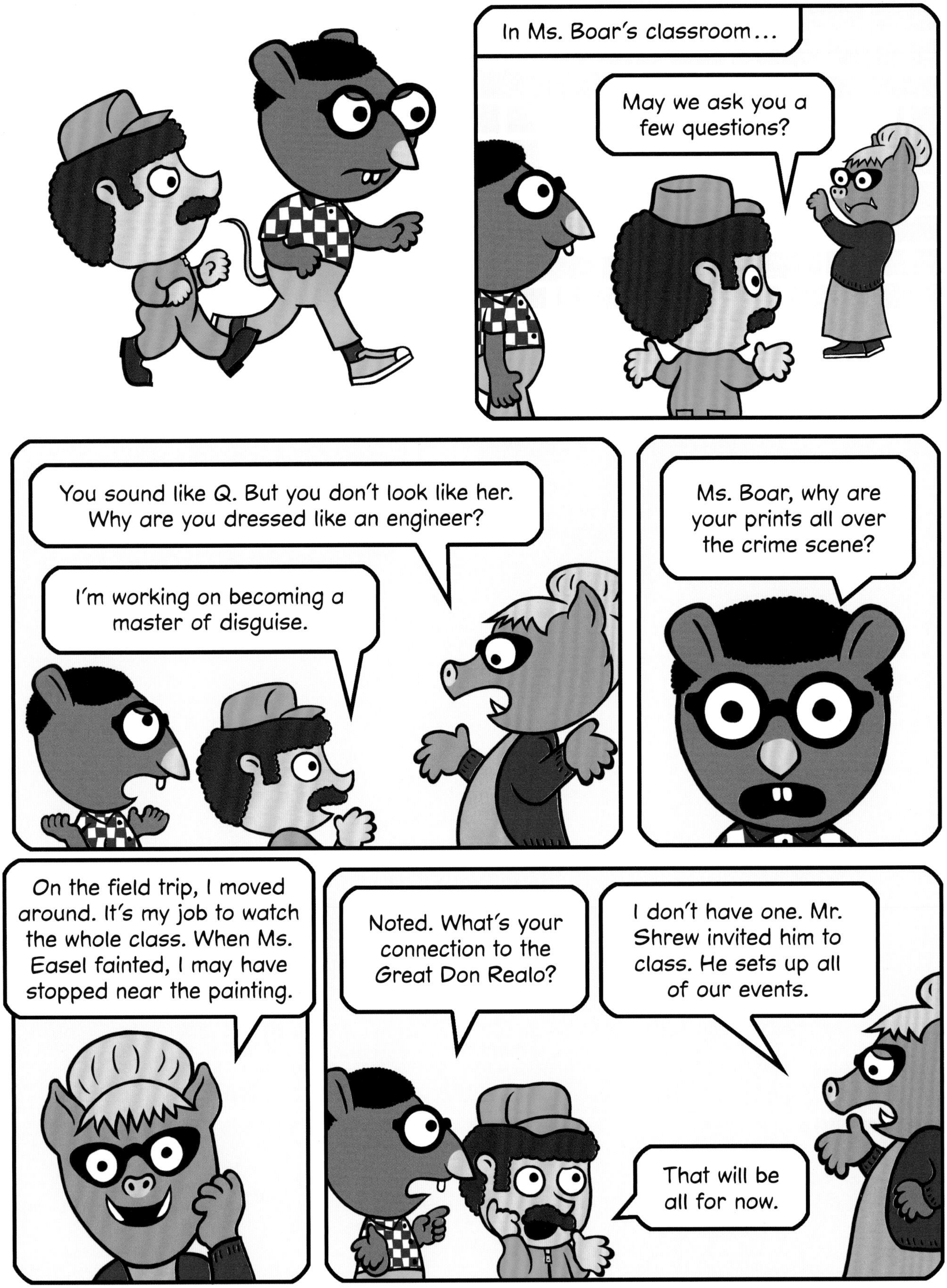
In Ms. Boar's classroom...
May we ask you a few questions?
You sound like Q. But you don't look like her. Why are you dressed like an engineer?
I'm working on becoming a master of disguise.
Ms. Boar, why are your prints all over the crime scene?
On the field trip, I moved around. It's my job to watch the whole class. When Ms. Easel fainted, I may have stopped near the painting.
Noted. What's your connection to the Great Don Realo?
I don't have one. Mr. Shrew invited him to class. He sets up all of our events.
That will be all for now.

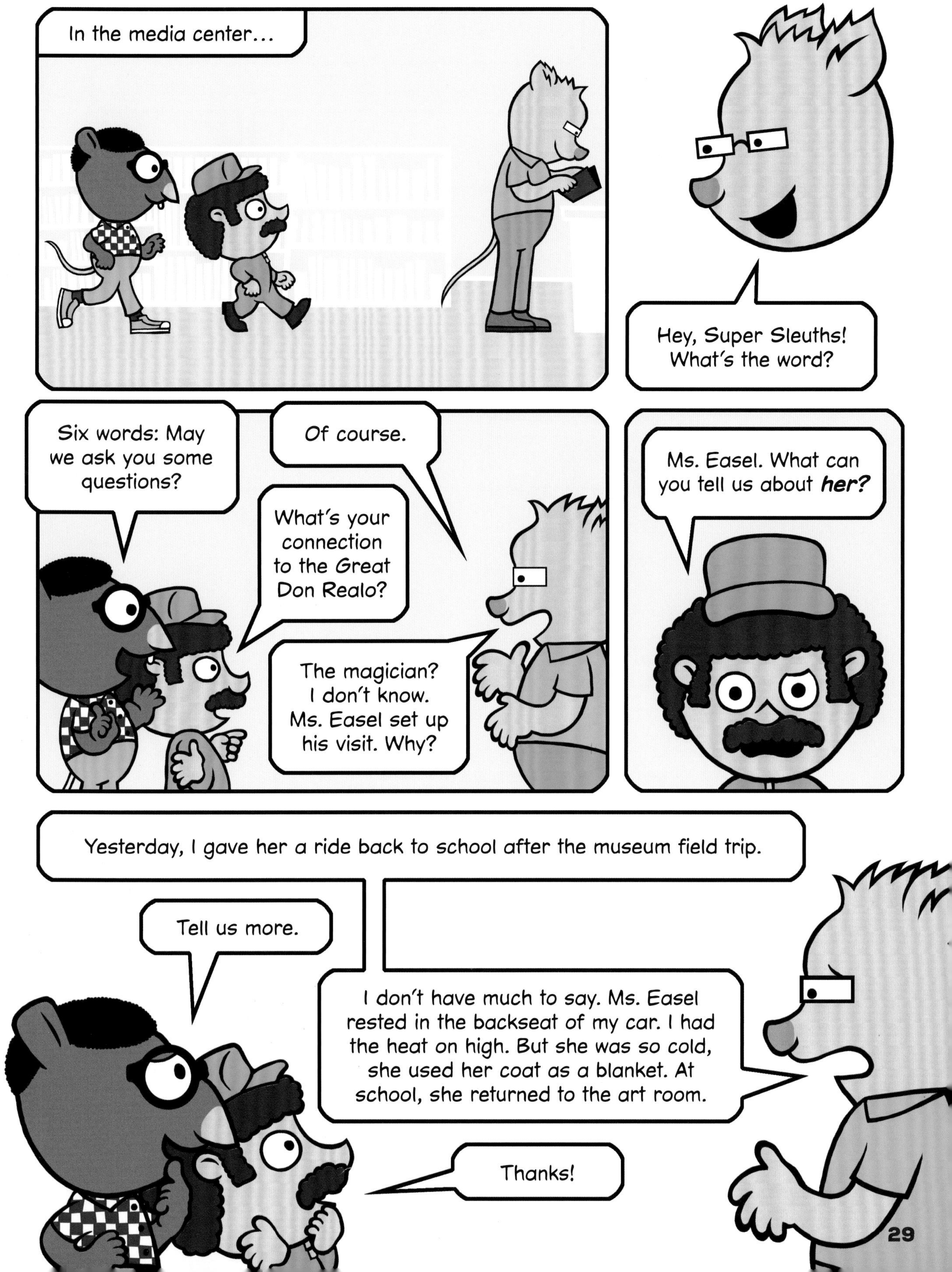

In the media center...
Hey, Super Sleuths! What's the word?
Six words: May we ask you some questions?
Of course.
What's your connection to the Great Don Realo?
The magician? I don't know. Ms. Easel set up his visit. Why?
Ms. Easel. What can you tell us about ***her?***
Yesterday, I gave her a ride back to school after the museum field trip.
Tell us more.
I don't have much to say. Ms. Easel rested in the backseat of my car. I had the heat on high. But she was so cold, she used her coat as a blanket. At school, she returned to the art room.
Thanks!

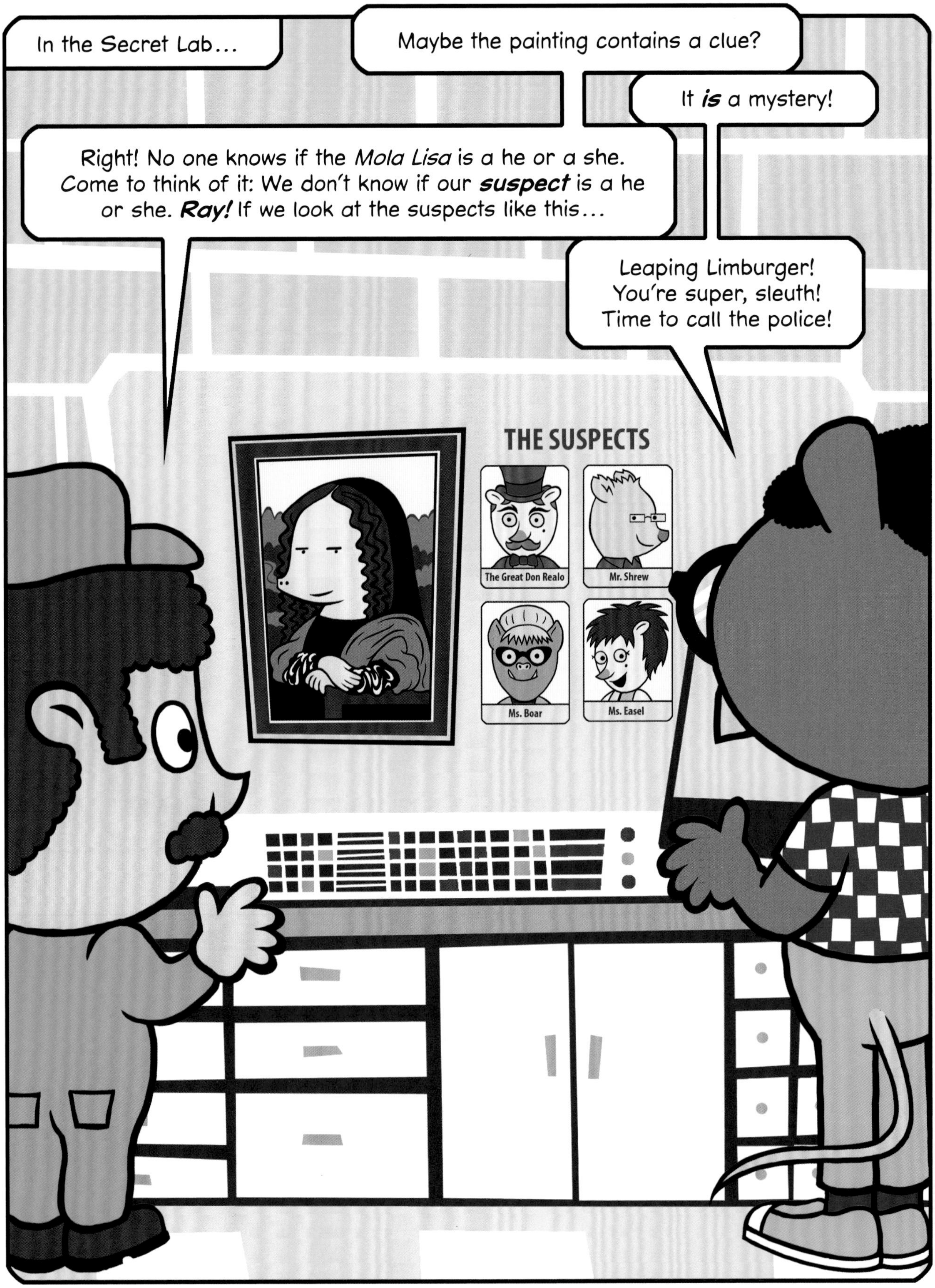
In the Secret Lab...
Maybe the painting contains a clue?
It *is* a mystery!
Right! No one knows if the *Mola Lisa* is a he or a she. Come to think of it: We don't know if our ***suspect*** is a he or she. ***Ray!*** If we look at the suspects like this...
Leaping Limburger! You're super, sleuth! Time to call the police!
THE SUSPECTS
The Great Don Realo
Mr. Shrew
Ms. Boar
Ms. Easel

CHAPTER SEVEN

The Great Don Revealo

In the art room...

Hello, Officer.

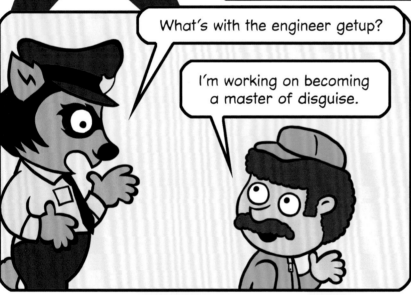

What's with the engineer getup?

I'm working on becoming a master of disguise.

Neat. You're well on your way.

What's the meaning of this? I need to prepare!

For an art class or a *magic show?*

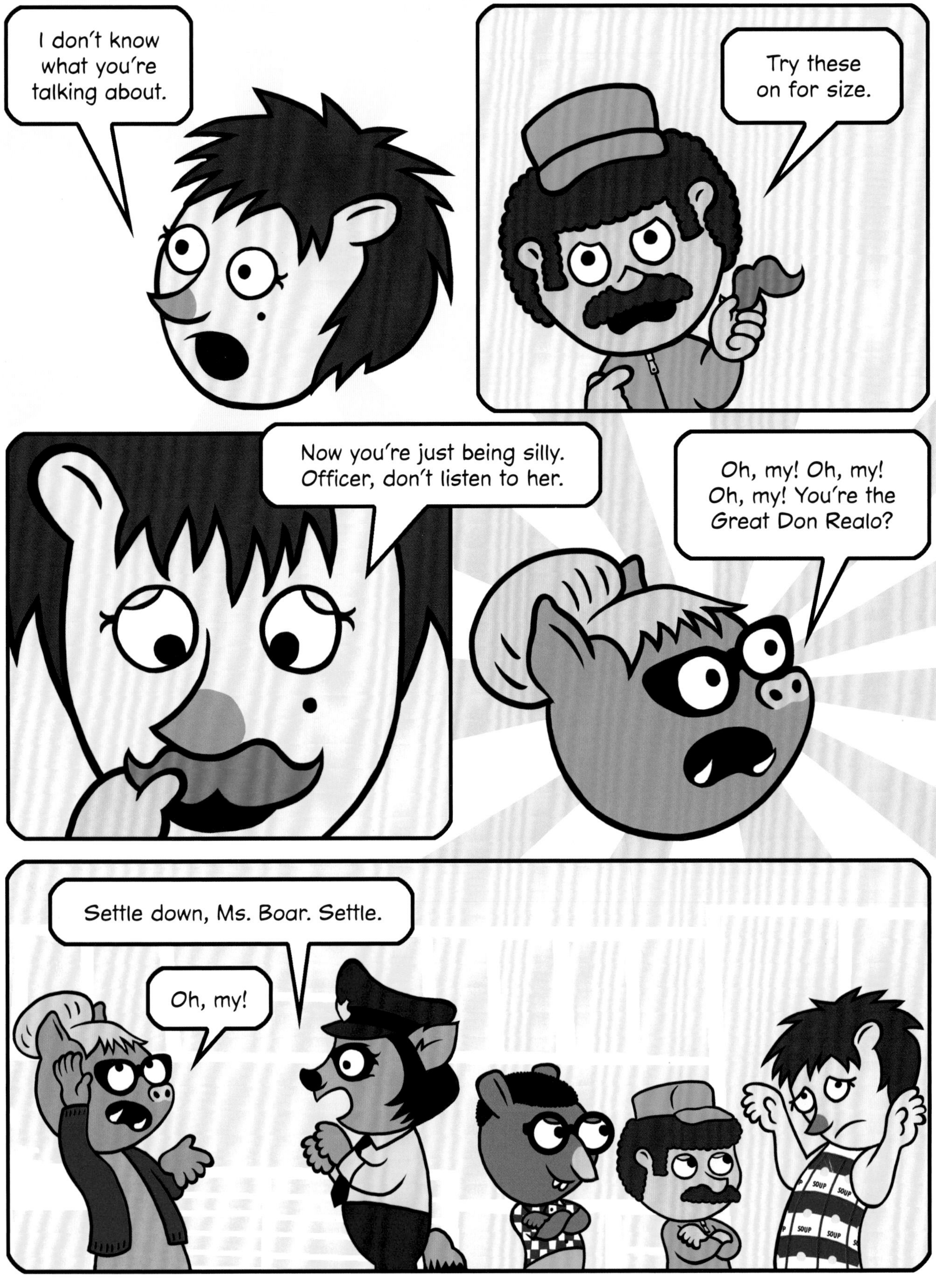
I don't know what you're talking about.
Try these on for size.
Now you're just being silly. Officer, don't listen to her.
Oh, my! Oh, my! Oh, my! You're the Great Don Realo?
Settle down, Ms. Boar. Settle.
Oh, my!
SOUP

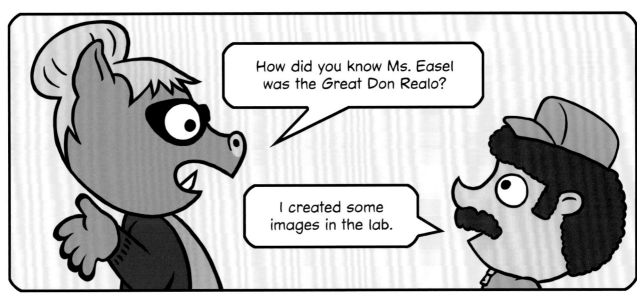

How did you know Ms. Easel was the Great Don Realo?

I created some images in the lab.

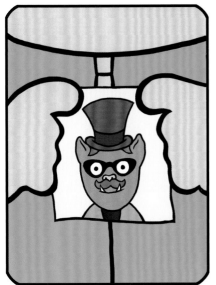

There's no law against dressing like a magician. But do you have proof she stole the painting?

Yesterday, the Great Don Realo performed a magic show for our class. And the painting thief was a true magician!

The lights went out at the art museum. Someone lit a flame. Someone yelled, "Fire." But it was a trick.

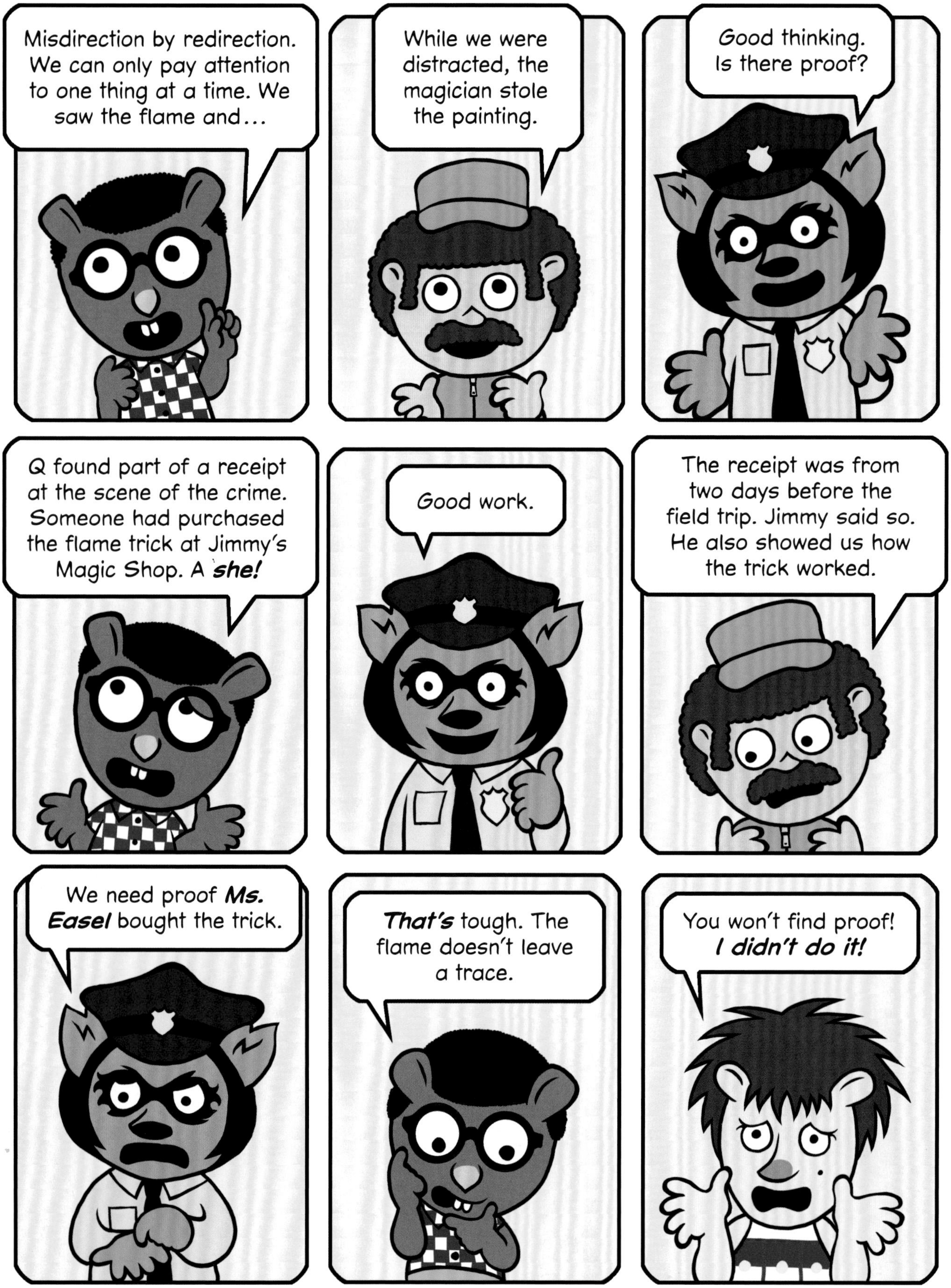
Misdirection by redirection. We can only pay attention to one thing at a time. We saw the flame and...
While we were distracted, the magician stole the painting.
Good thinking. Is there proof?
Q found part of a receipt at the scene of the crime. Someone had purchased the flame trick at Jimmy's Magic Shop. A *she!*
Good work.
The receipt was from two days before the field trip. Jimmy said so. He also showed us how the trick worked.
We need proof ***Ms. Easel*** bought the trick.
That's tough. The flame doesn't leave a trace.
You won't find proof! ***I didn't do it!***

How about this? At the end of Realo's act, confetti fell.

Ray found the same confetti at the scene of the crime.

A student could have dropped it.

Can I go now?

After stealing the painting, Ms. Easel pretended to faint.

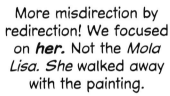

More misdirection by redirection! We focused on *her.* Not the *Mola Lisa. She* walked away with the painting.

How?

We're not exactly sure...

Sorry, sleuths. We can't hold her without proof.

CHAPTER EIGHT

More Magic

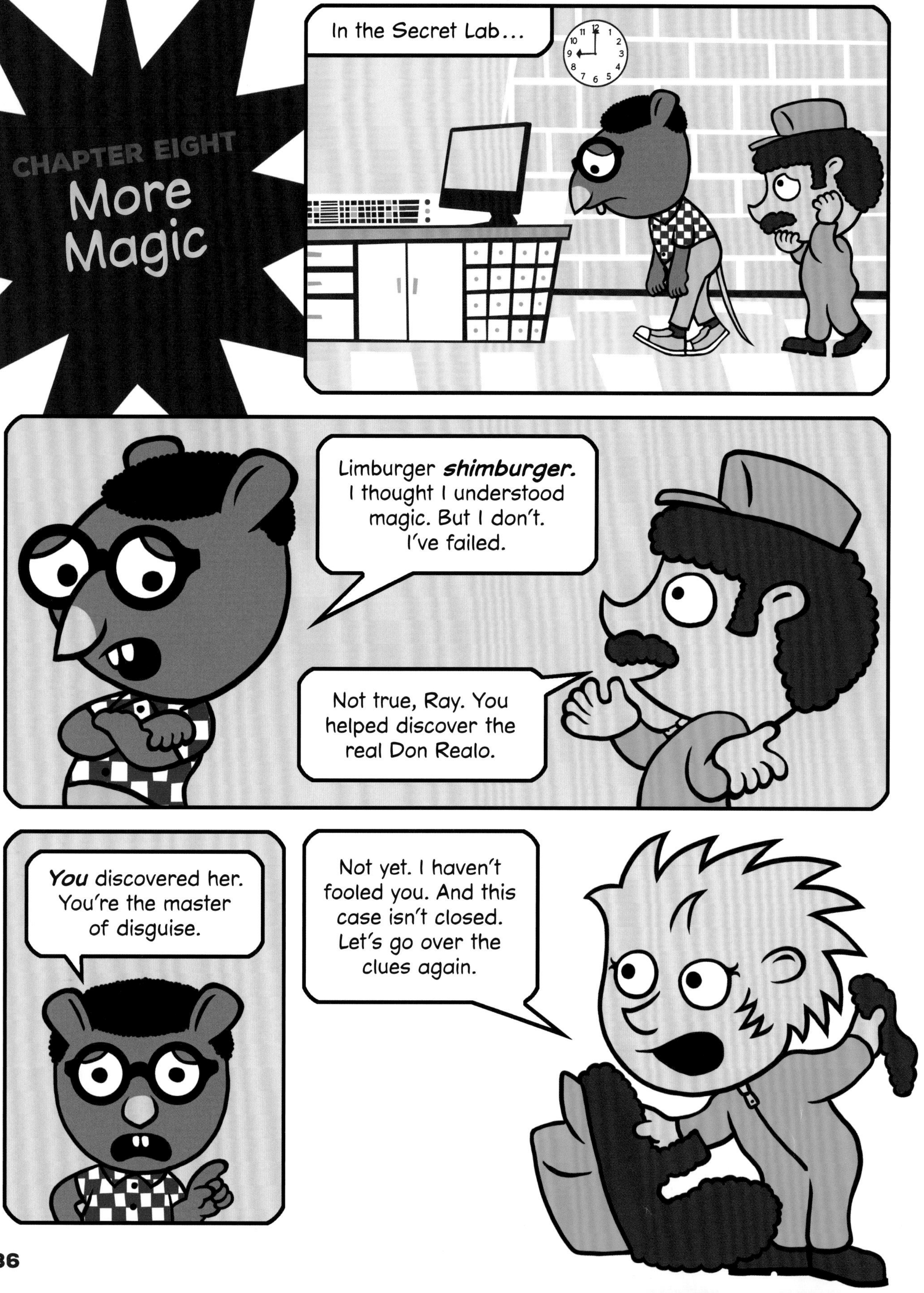
In the Secret Lab...
Limburger *shimburger.* I thought I understood magic. But I don't. I've failed.
Not true, Ray. You helped discover the real Don Realo.
You discovered her. You're the master of disguise.
Not yet. I haven't fooled you. And this case isn't closed. Let's go over the clues again.

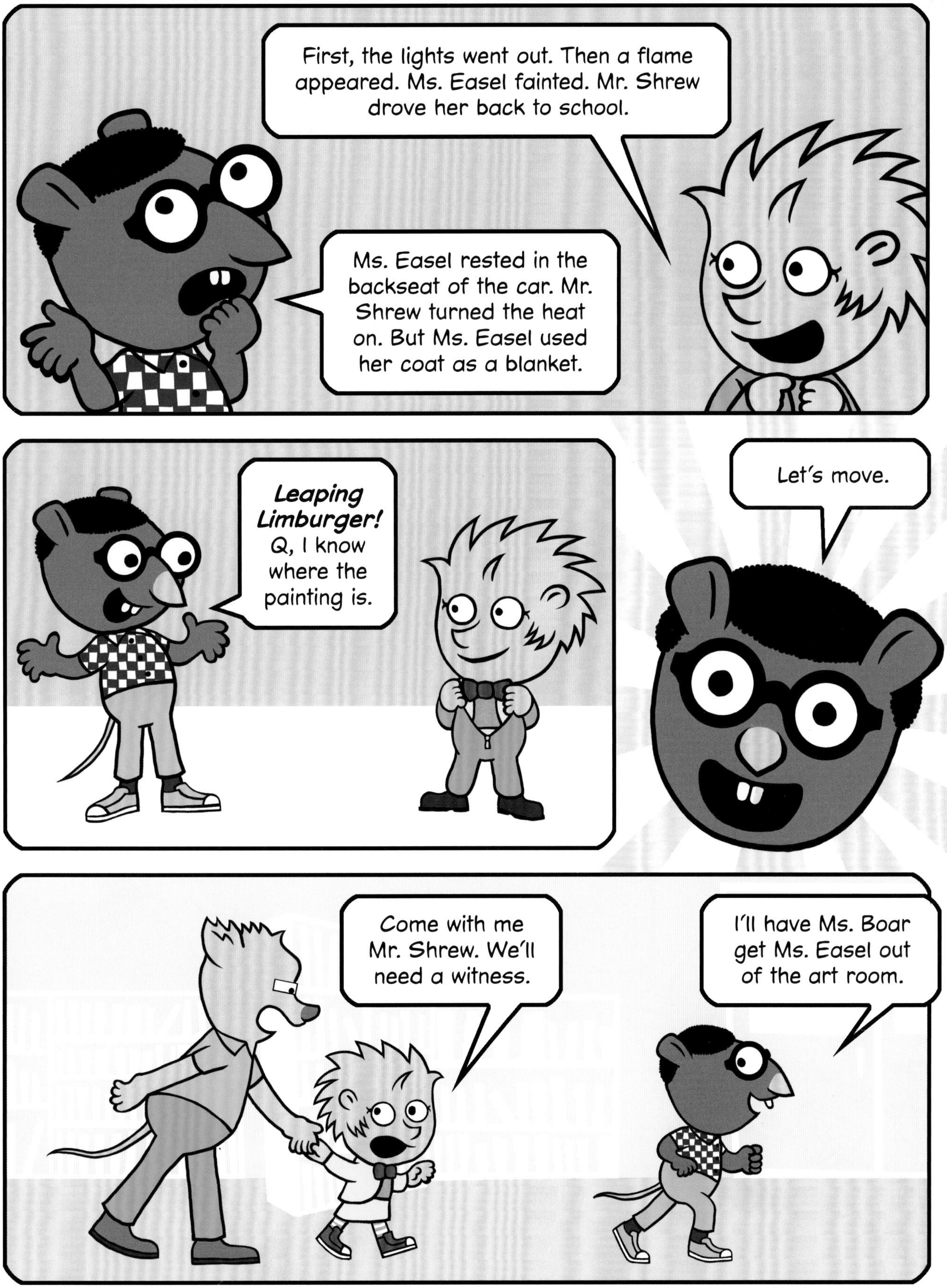
First, the lights went out. Then a flame appeared. Ms. Easel fainted. Mr. Shrew drove her back to school.
Ms. Easel rested in the backseat of the car. Mr. Shrew turned the heat on. But Ms. Easel used her coat as a blanket.
Leaping Limburger! Q, I know where the painting is.
Let's move.
Come with me Mr. Shrew. We'll need a witness.
I'll have Ms. Boar get Ms. Easel out of the art room.

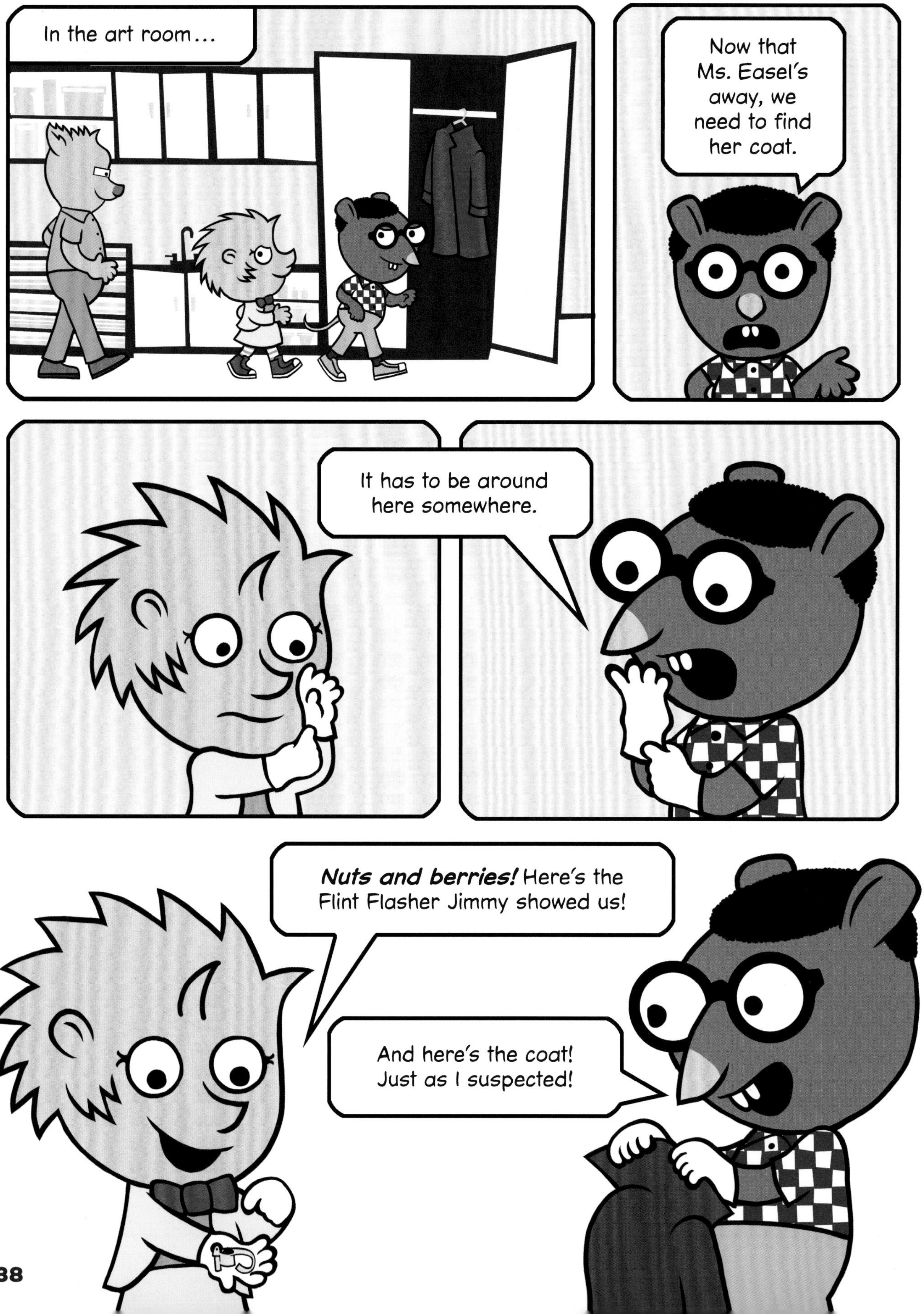
In the art room...
Now that Ms. Easel's away, we need to find her coat.
It has to be around here somewhere.
Nuts and berries! Here's the Flint Flasher Jimmy showed us!
And here's the coat! Just as I suspected!

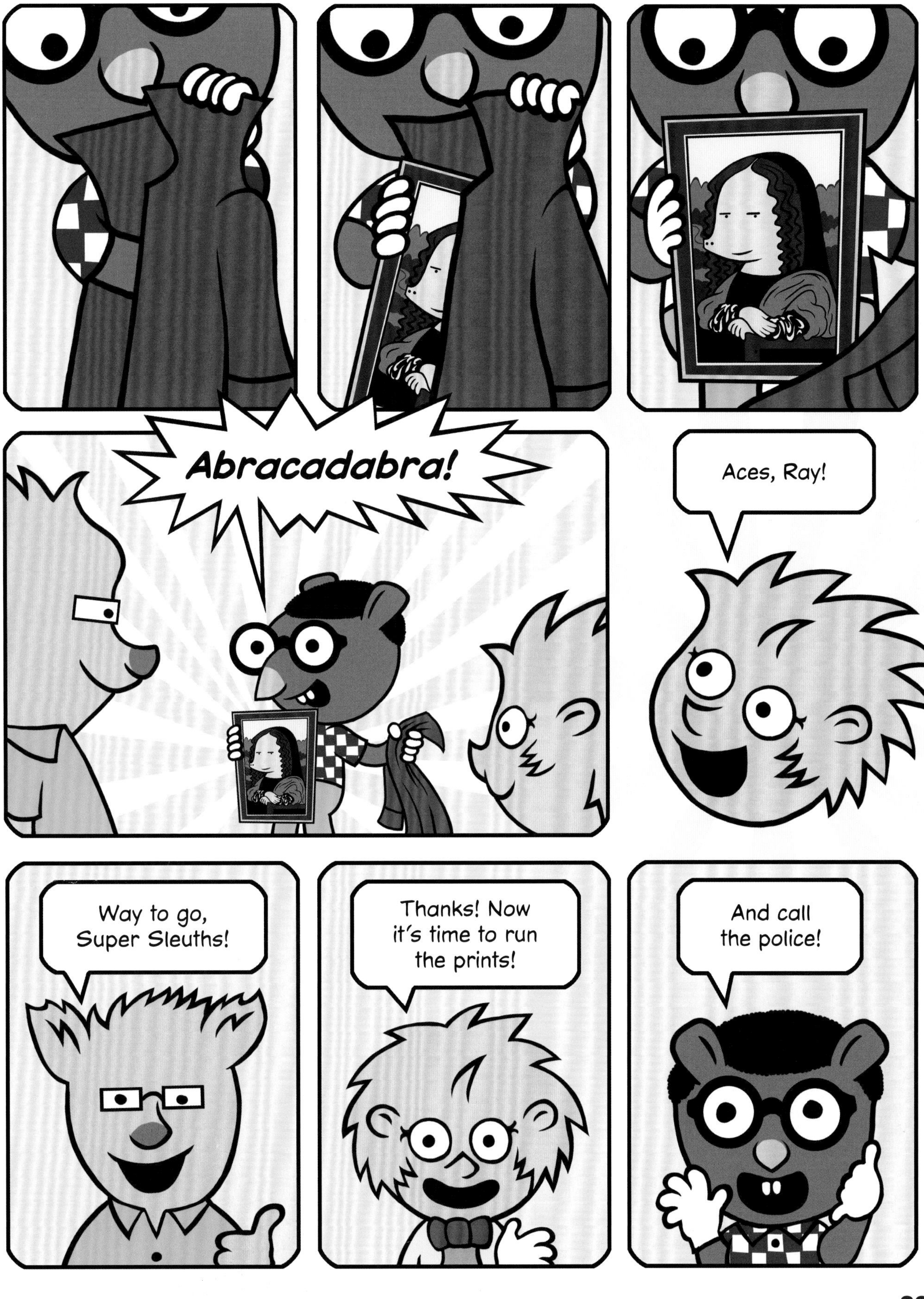
Abracadabra!
Aces, Ray!
Way to go, Super Sleuths!
Thanks! Now it's time to run the prints!
And call the police!

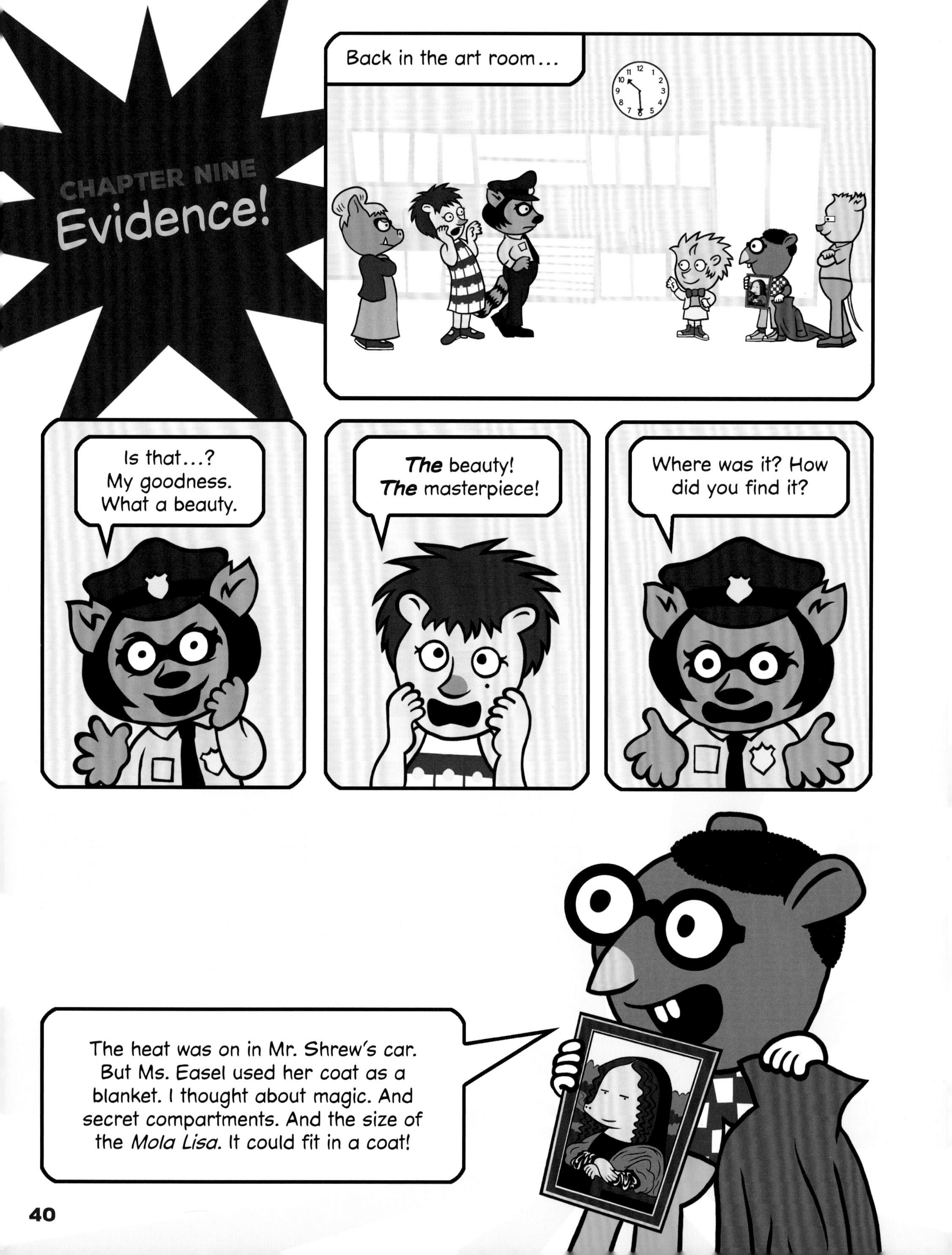
CHAPTER NINE
Evidence!
Back in the art room...
Is that...? My goodness. What a beauty.
The beauty! *The* masterpiece!
Where was it? How did you find it?
The heat was on in Mr. Shrew's car. But Ms. Easel used her coat as a blanket. I thought about magic. And secret compartments. And the size of the *Mola Lisa*. It could fit in a coat!

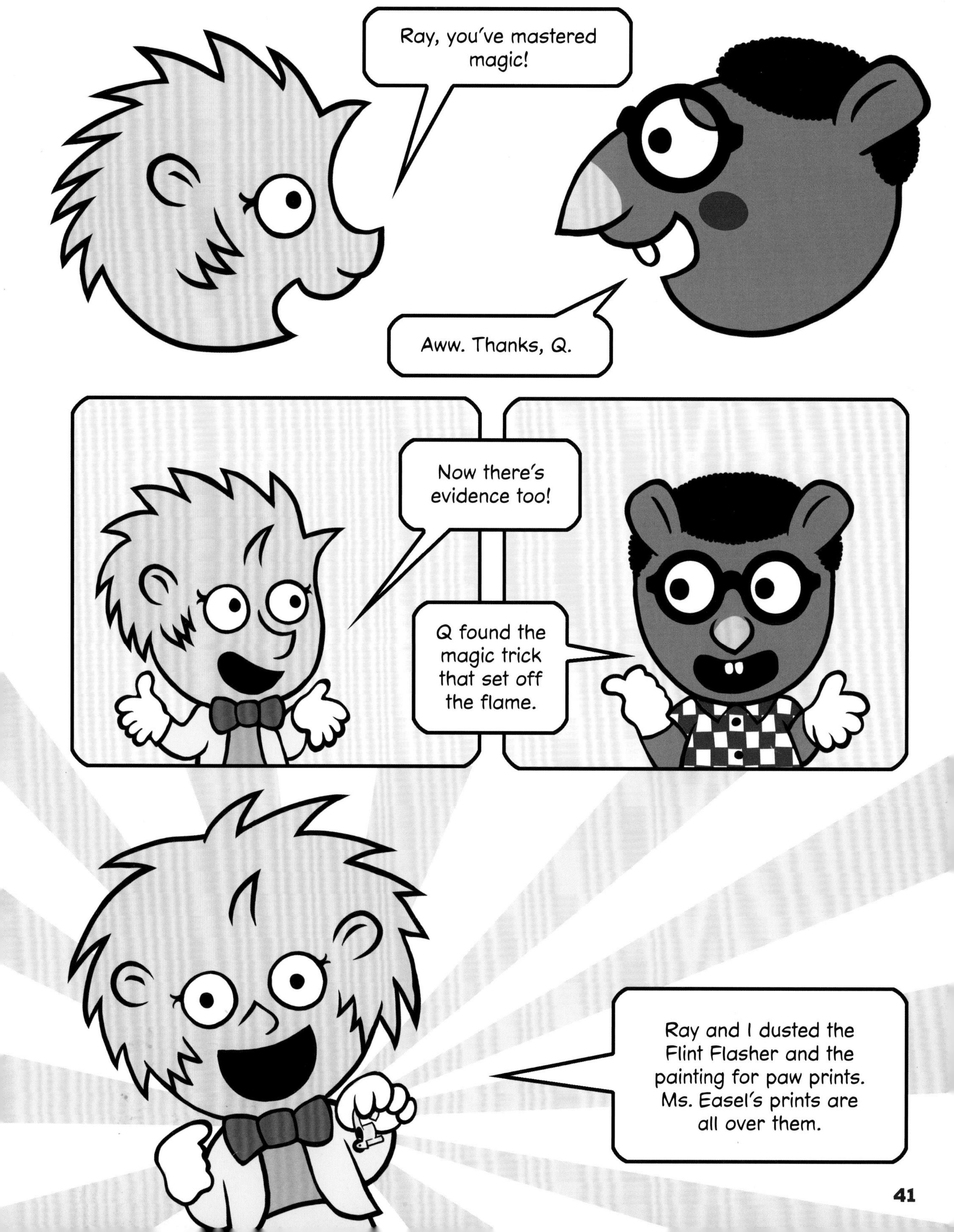
Ray, you've mastered magic!
Aww. Thanks, Q.
Now there's evidence too!
Q found the magic trick that set off the flame.
Ray and I dusted the Flint Flasher and the painting for paw prints. Ms. Easel's prints are all over them.

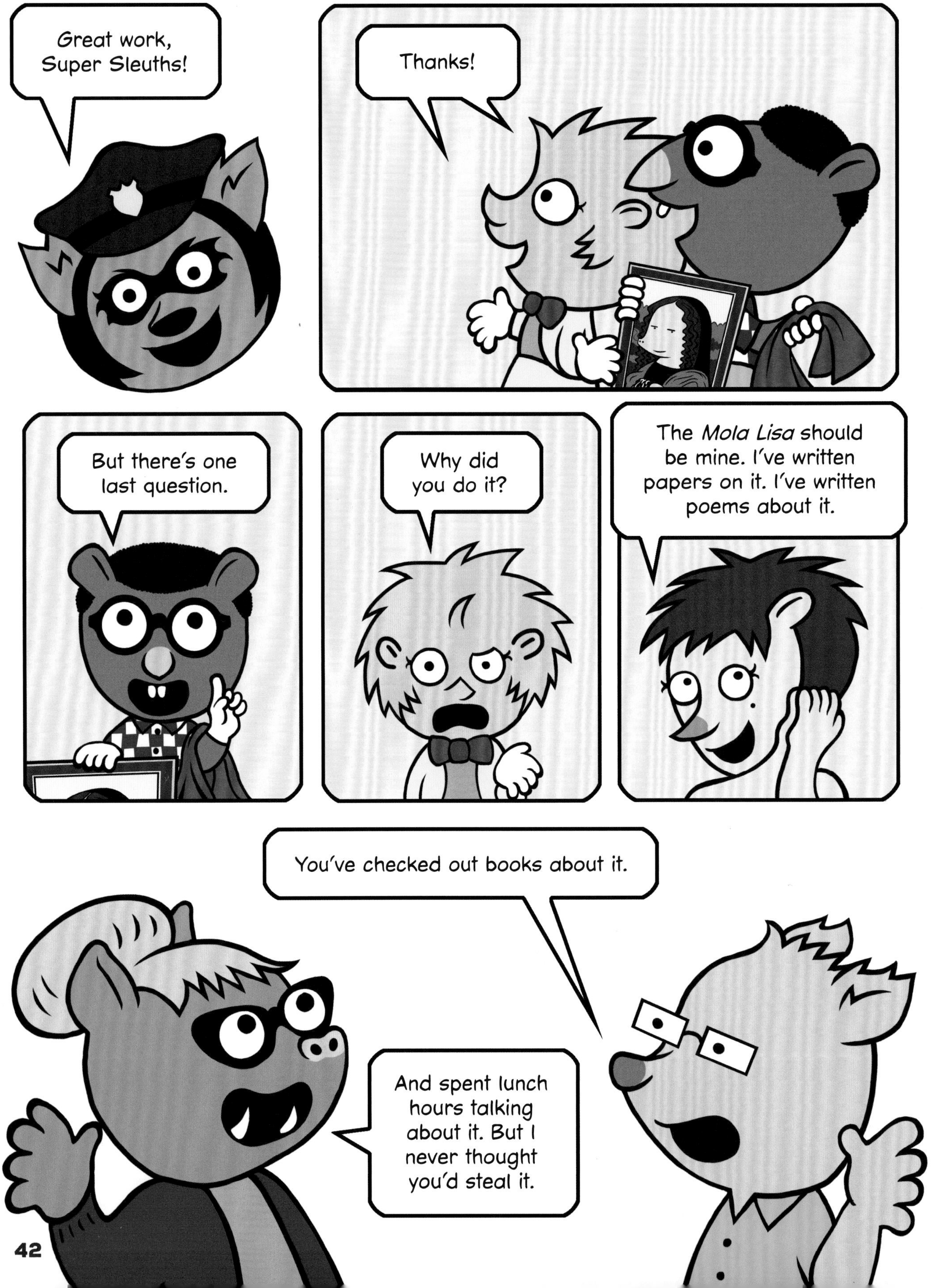
Great work, Super Sleuths!
Thanks!
But there's one last question.
Why did you do it?
The *Mola Lisa* should be mine. I've written papers on it. I've written poems about it.
You've checked out books about it.
And spent lunch hours talking about it. But I never thought you'd steal it.

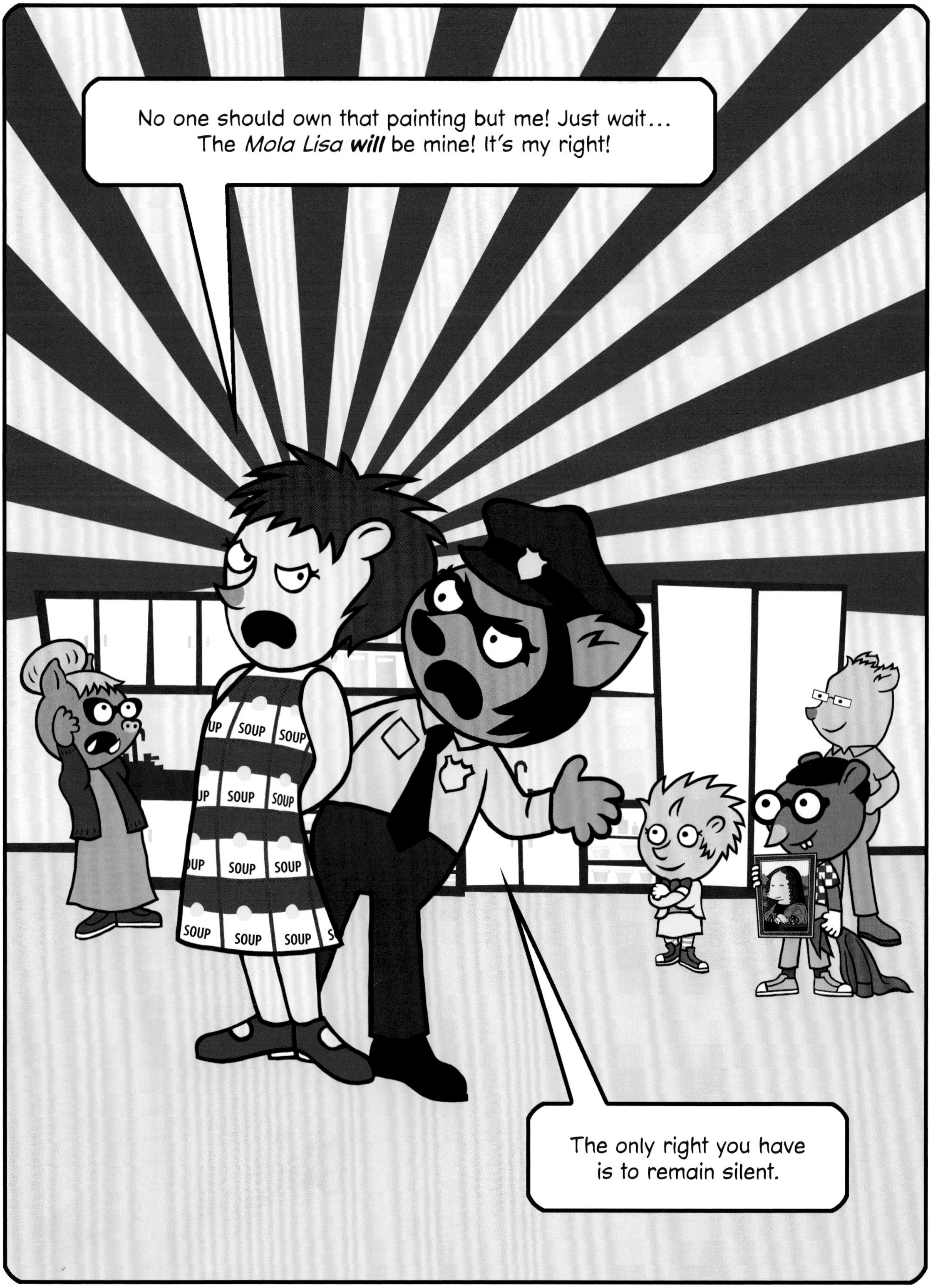
No one should own that painting but me! Just wait... The *Mola Lisa* ***will*** be mine! It's my right!
SOUP
The only right you have is to remain silent.

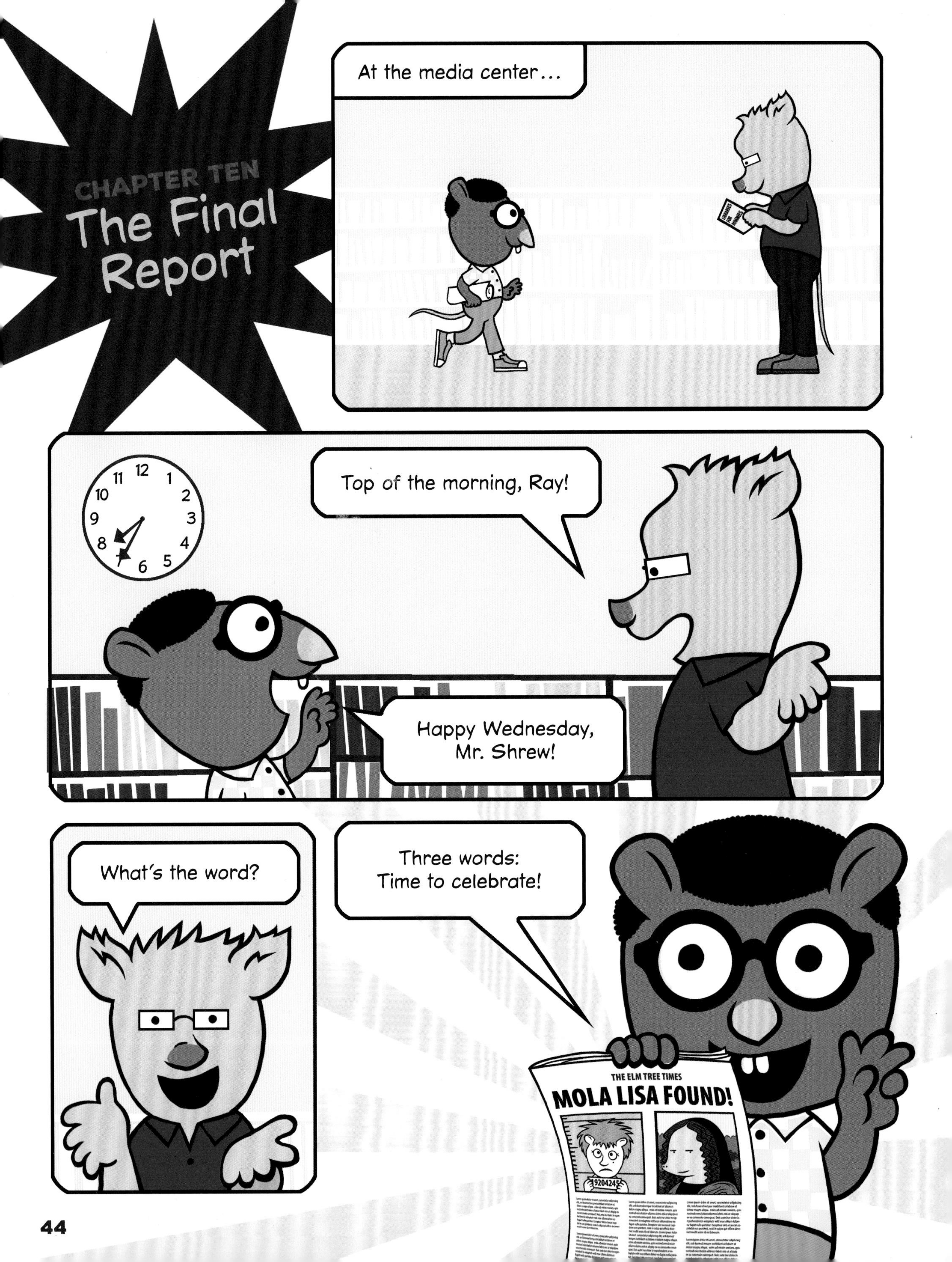
CHAPTER TEN
The Final Report
At the media center...
LIBRARIES FOR DUMMIES
Top of the morning, Ray!
Happy Wednesday, Mr. Shrew!
What's the word?
Three words: Time to celebrate!
THE ELM TREE TIMES
MOLA LISA FOUND!
9204245

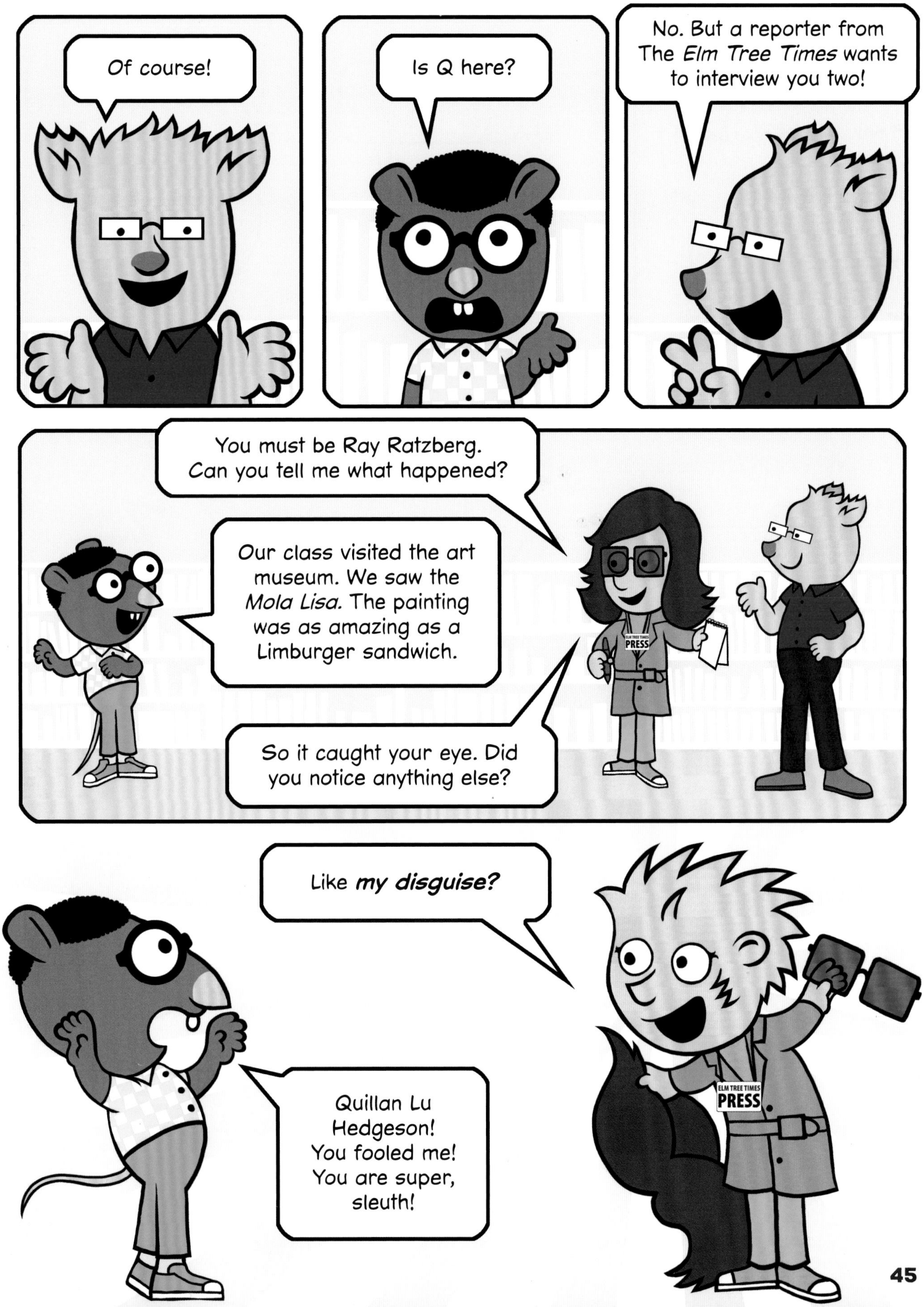
Of course!
Is Q here?
No. But a reporter from The *Elm Tree Times* wants to interview you two!
You must be Ray Ratzberg. Can you tell me what happened?
Our class visited the art museum. We saw the *Mola Lisa.* The painting was as amazing as a Limburger sandwich.
ELM TREE TIMES PRESS
So it caught your eye. Did you notice anything else?
Like ***my disguise?***
Quillan Lu Hedgeson! You fooled me! You are super, sleuth!
ELM TREE TIMES PRESS

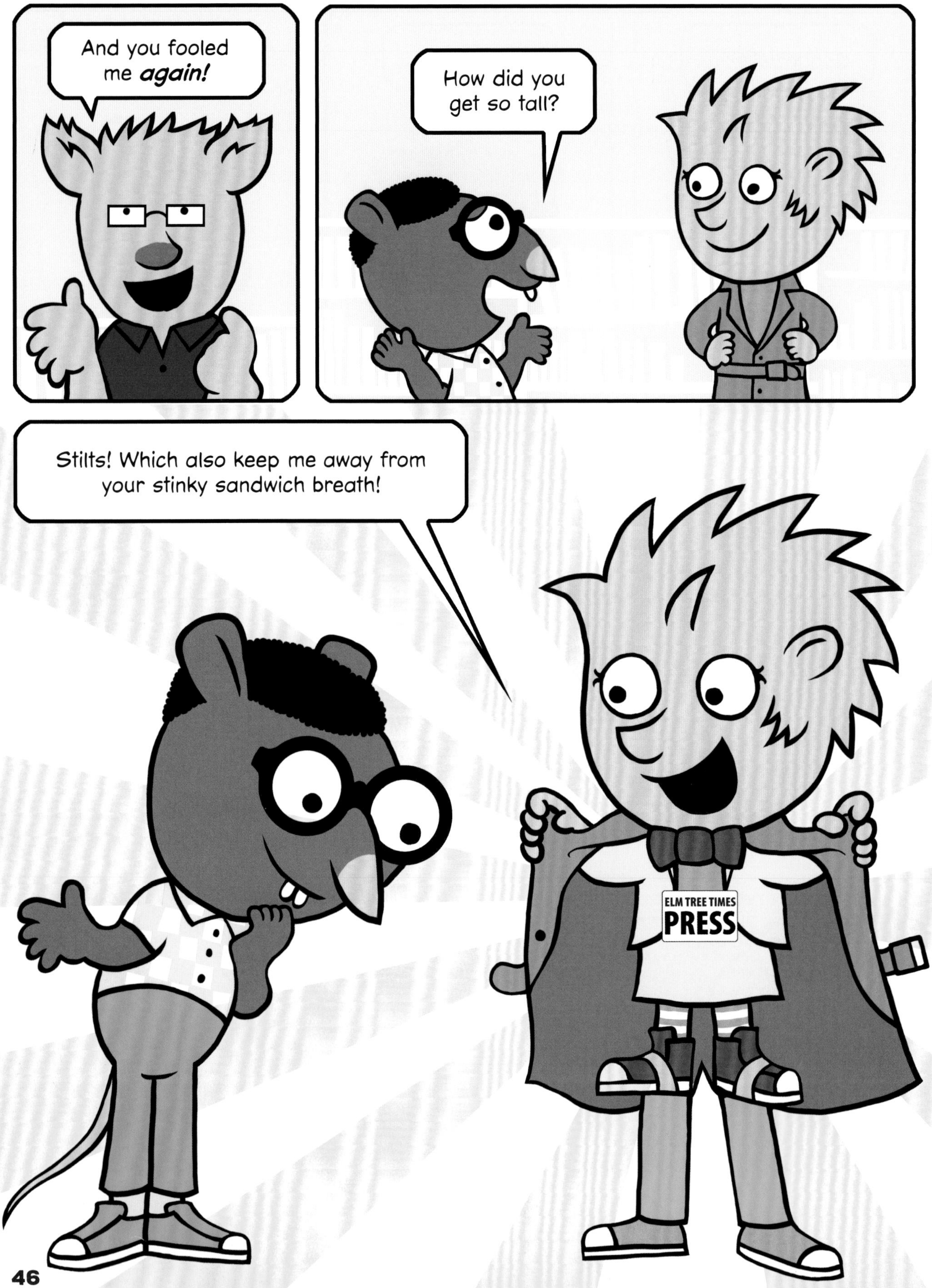
And you fooled me *again!*
How did you get so tall?
Stilts! Which also keep me away from your stinky sandwich breath!
ELM TREE TIMES PRESS

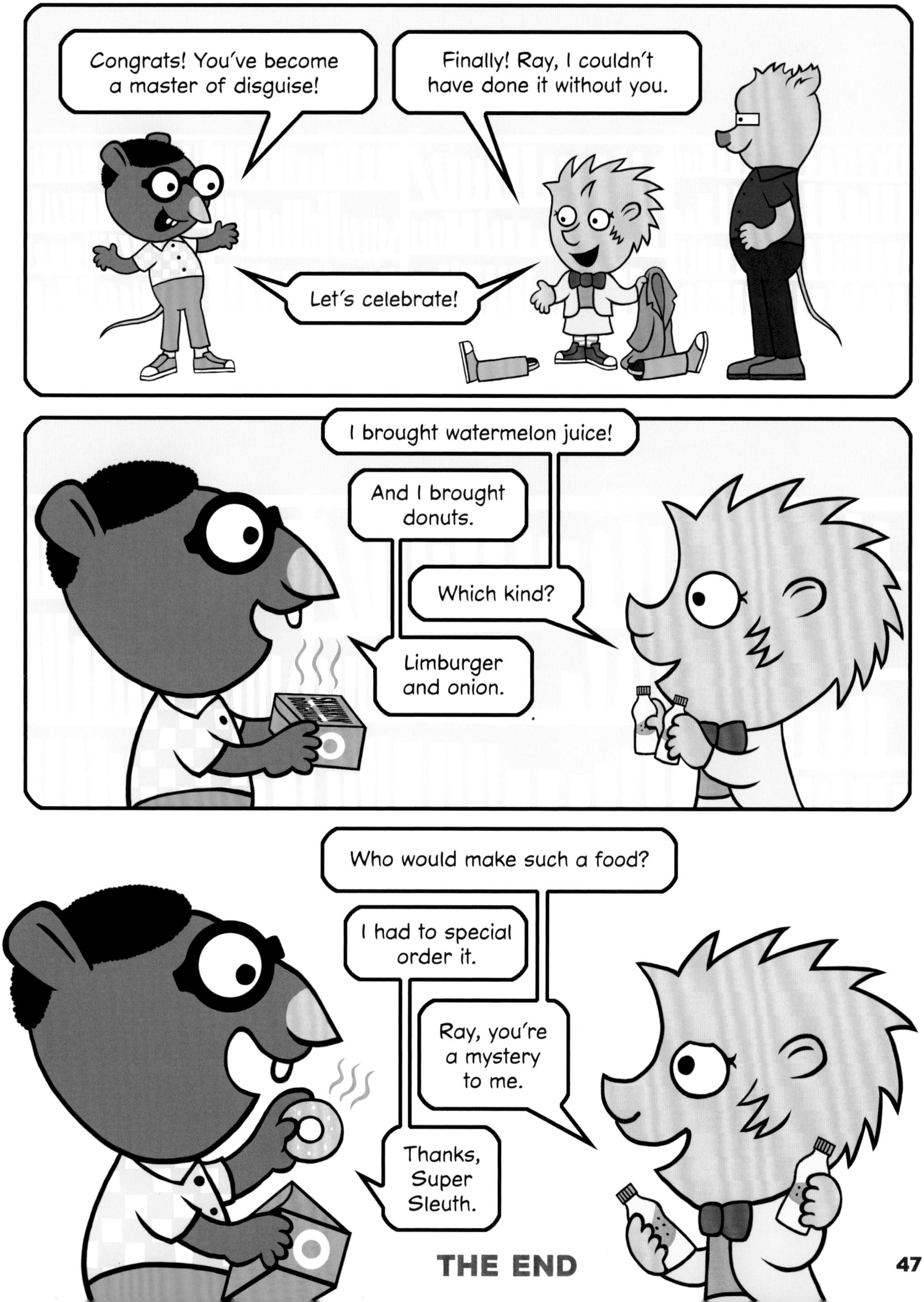
Congrats! You've become a master of disguise!
Finally! Ray, I couldn't have done it without you.
Let's celebrate!
I brought watermelon juice!
And I brought donuts.
Which kind?
Limburger and onion.
Who would make such a food?
I had to special order it.
Ray, you're a mystery to me.
Thanks, Super Sleuth.
THE END

ABOUT THE AUTHOR

Trisha Speed Shaskan has written more than forty books for children, including her latest picture book, *Punk Skunks*, illustrated by her husband Stephen Shaskan. She received her MFA in creative writing from Minnesota State University, Mankato. She has taught creative writing to students at every level from kindergarten to graduate school. She is super excited to have written her first graphic novel because one of her childhood heroes was—and still is—Wonder Woman. The couple live in Minneapolis, Minnesota, with their dog, Bea, and their cat, Eartha, named after Eartha Kitt, famous for her role as Catwoman.

ABOUT THE ILLUSTRATOR

Stephen Shaskan is the author and illustrator of *A Dog Is a Dog*, *Max Speed*, *The Three Triceratops Tuff*, and *Toad on the Road: A Cautionary Tale*. He's the illustrator of *Punk Skunks* too, a book written by his wife, Trisha Speed Shaskan. He's also a graduate of the Rhode Island School of Design, an early childhood educator, and a music maker. And he is super excited to be creating his first graphic novel, since he grew up collecting comic books in upstate New York. He lives in Minneapolis, Minnesota, with his wife, Trisha Speed Shaskan, their cat, Eartha, and their dog, Bea. Visit him at stephenshaskan.com.

FUN FACTS

LEONARDO DA VINCI

Leonardo da Squinty is based on **Leonardo da Vinci**.

Leonardo da Vinci was born in 1452 in Italy. Growing up, da Vinci only learned basic reading, writing, and math. But he was a talented artist. His father had him study under a noted sculptor and painter for ten years. At twenty-six years old, da Vinci became a master himself. Four years later, he moved to Milan, Italy. He worked as an engineer and painter. He was also an architect and designer of court festivals.

He lived during a period called the Renaissance (1300–1600). It was a time of great learning in Europe. Many people explored art, science, and literature. Leonardo da Vinci's ideas were way ahead of his time. He made designs that looked like a modern hang glider, a helicopter, and a bicycle.

He was always curious. He wondered why light came from the moon. He wondered why the sky was blue. He used art to explore his questions. His most famous "experiment" is the *Mona Lisa*. It became the most famous painting in the world. And it inspired the *Mola Lisa* too!